A DEV__   E

A Saint-Emilion Vineyard Mystery

Patrick Hilyer

There is a devil in every berry of the grape.

Turkish proverb

What are memories but stories we tell ourselves about the past? And, like stories, memories can change with each retelling. Some need to be put away and forgotten, but others need to be written down, fixed in time, recorded; otherwise they alter or fade or get lost forever. My frustrating experiences in the witness box have taught me that, if nothing else.

Now, as I look back at last summer, the disastrous date with Captain Lefèvre and the horrific discovery of the corpse in the wine vat are mere memories; so too is the fortnight of emotional maelstroms that followed. Now, looking out at my vineyard and its rows of bare, frozen vines, I know who did it. I know who killed René Rougeard.

But I mustn't get ahead of myself. I need to relate the events as I experienced them, write it all down, build the suspense, collect the facts as they drip from the winepress of my memory before, like last time, they seep away. Last time my memories were unreliable, and so was my testimony. This time I need to get my story straight, even if no one outside the courtroom ever hears it. Who knows, perhaps someone might actually enjoy reading it? Ah, but I can just imagine my father's sardonic response to that: *so now you're a writer are you, Jeanie? A failed law student; a widowed winemaker; an amateur sleuth who got shot in the neck on her first case; and now a writer!*

Okay, Dad, I may have failed at many things, but I do have a story to tell. So I'll continue, if you don't mind.

Dimanche 4 Séptembre 2011

It's just before dawn, and the lights are out in this wing of the hospital. Urged on by a devil, the young man gropes his way through the darkness, a room key clutched in one shaky hand, a syringe in the other. He pushes the devil away, unlocks the door and enters. In the dim light that filters through the window's metal grille he can see her, asleep on the bed: his girl, his beautiful girl, the girl who killed their child.

In her dream there are devils too; and there, amid a chorus of hellish cries, she hears the young man's voice.

'Marguerite?'

She feels the touch of his cold hand on hers.

'Is that you, *mon cheri?*'

He has found her at last. He will save her, take her away from this place. She's no longer scared, not even of death. She loves him, and he loves her.

'It's me, *cherie*,' he replies.

The drug is still with her, in her blood, in her brain. Her memories carry her back to the dirty backstreet where they first met, to the moment when their hands first touched. He was so gentle then, so kind. Does he remember?

He speaks again, more urgently. 'We have to go – now.'

She recalls the *jardin public* where they used to meet at dusk, the smell of springtime blossom.

'Come on!'

He tries to lift her, but she won't move. She must be

crazy. He switches on the bedside lamp, illuminating the face of the devil who urges him to do what he must do – quickly.

Slowly she sits up in bed and opens her arms, palms up. 'The devil!' she gasps. 'Can you see his burning eyes?'

He fastens a tourniquet round her upper arm. *Go on, save her,* his devil says.

'Oh God, help me, please,' she cries as the needle slides into her soft flesh.

He withdraws the needle, turns away from her and injects his own arm.

She's delirious. 'I can see the angels,' she says.

He reaches out to embrace her.

'Your hands!' she cries. 'So stained with blood!'

She's finished, says the devil, leaving the room.

'Saved,' the young man whispers.

She falls back gently against the white pillow; he slips down onto the cold tiles.

An alarm bell rings. The stage lights come on.

I suppose I'm an old-fashioned kind of girl. Okay, so I'm not exactly a girl any more. I may still feel twenty-two, but I only have to look in the mirror to remind myself that a quarter of a century has passed since I came to Saint-Emilion. Still, all those years spent turning grapes into wine haven't been too unkind to me. Like my '95s, I think I've aged fairly well.

So, not old, but definitely old-fashioned. For me, the opera should be all gorgeous frocks, flamboyant scenery and men in tights. Not that I was complaining – I hadn't paid for the tickets after all. But a modern adaptation of Gounod's *Faust* set in the juvenile wing of a psychiatric hospital just wasn't my cup of tea. Hospitals are among the few things I can't stand – along with snakes, guns, early morning confrontations, goodbyes, pruning my vines . . . well, there are lots of things I dislike, but hospitals are the worst.

At least Pierre had been there, sitting beside me.

Pierre Lefèvre: the man who'd saved my life, the softly spoken police captain whose thigh, when it touched mine in the near-darkness of the auditorium, had sent my pulse racing.

Admittedly, the opera wasn't all bad. The music was sublime, and by portraying Mephistopheles as a figment of Faust's drug-addled mind, the Austrian baritone had given a convincing devil. I shuddered, recalling his dark, gaunt features, blood-red eyes and the spike of crimson hair crowning his sallow, shaven head.

I empathised with Faust. There was a time when I had my own demons to cope with. One in particular, whom I called my evil gremlin, would never leave me alone. But, strangely, after being shot in the neck I haven't heard from him since. Now I talk to my Jack Russell terrier instead. He doesn't talk back.

Of course, I empathised most strongly with the poor girl, Marguerite. I never did have children of my own, and now, halfway down life's one-way street, I've accepted I never will. A couple of years ago I resolved to help the young people around me, knowing that there are more than enough children in the world. Knowing is one thing; feeling is quite another.

I was delighted with the venue for our post-matinee dinner. Lefèvre had managed to get a table at Bordeaux's best – well, second-best – restaurant. Earlier, I'd been apprehensive, this being my first date since Andrew had passed away a year and a half earlier, but now I was beginning to relax and enjoy the evening.

Apart from at my partner's funeral, I'd worn nothing but a pair of old jeans and a flannel shirt for the past two years. This evening I had on a black dress, black heels and my last pair of sheer tights. The dress felt a tad more figure-hugging than the last time I'd dressed for dinner, and the shoes were killing my feet, but it felt good to be there in the restaurant's cavernous dining room, anticipating a delicious, gastronomic dinner surrounded by

4

Bordeaux's bourgeoisie.

Lefèvre hailed the waiter and ordered champagne. I tried not to look at the stratospheric prices on the menu and, instead, took in my surroundings. Everything about the place merited the chef's two Michelin stars. The table, like the décor, was impeccable. No wrinkle dared show itself on the perfect white table cloth on top of which the squeaky-clean crystal glasses, linen napkins, and elegant silverware had been arranged with pinpoint precision. Pink roses, still bearing the morning's dew, formed the centrepiece. The *assiettes de presentation*, I noticed, turning mine over, were Limoges. The other diners, like us, were mostly in their forties and fifties. I reasoned that few young people or pensioners could afford such a swanky place.

The waiter served our drinks, and we toasted each other's health.

'*A votre santé.*'

Police Captain Pierre Lefèvre and I have known each other for three years but we've never settled on a mutually agreeable language. When speaking French we've always used the formal *vous* form of address which doesn't suit me at all. English is my preference – it's far less starchy.

Lefèvre took a sip of his champagne then looked at me, smiling.

'*Merci, Jeanne,*' – at least he'd stopped calling me *madame* – 'and sorry for . . . you know.'

I understood the apology: we'd lost a murder conviction. But he had no need to thank me. 'No, thank *you*. You saved my life remember?'

He eyed the fizzy contents of his fluted glass. 'Oh, not really. You made sure everything worked out fine.'

'But if you hadn't turned up when you did—'

'—then we would not have made the drugs haul, I would not have got a promotion, and we would not be here enjoying these expensive aperitifs.'

Should I have offered to go Dutch? Oh please, I thought, don't let him be a cheapskate.

'Pride comes before a fall,' I said, teasing.

His smile faded. 'You know, in my line of work that is not an expression we like to use.'

He didn't need to explain. I'd been on the receiving end of a pistol barrel only once in my life but, for Captain Lefèvre, getting shot was a daily hazard.

'No, sorry.' I raised my glass. 'Let's drink to your success.'

The smile returned. 'And to yours, too, Jeanne.'

Now how the hell did he know about that?

I'd barely begun to peruse the list of delicious-sounding hors d'oeuvres when Lefèvre's phone buzzed.

'Let me take this call, then you can tell me how terrible the opera was.'

He picked-up, gave his name. His expression said bad news.

'Where? . . . In a what? . . . *Merde*. Okay, I will be there as soon as I— . . . No, I am in the city . . . What's the ad—? . . . But that's in the Dordogne, *n'est-ce pas*? . . . No, of course not, I can be there within the hour . . . No, he's still on vacation . . .'

He closed the flap of the phone and frowned. 'I am sorry, Jeanne.'

'What is it?'

'Something has come up. I have to go.'

'But you haven't eaten—'

'A body has been found, north of Libourne.'

Adrenalin replaced the empty feeling in my stomach.

'Oh, I see. Well, of course I understand.'

He'd already put on his jacket and waved a twenty euro note to signal for the bill. I stood up and picked up my handbag. Lefèvre flashed his police ID card at the waiter, mumbled his excuses and left the bank note on the man's tray. Then, as we made our way to the door, Lefèvre related the scant details he'd been given by his boss.

'A winemaker has been found dead in one of his vats, Jeanne. It does not look like an accident.'

My God, I thought, how awful.

'Oh, dear. Can you drop me off on the way?'

He stopped on the pavement outside.

'Er, there is not enough time. Perhaps you could come with me? I might need your expertise.'

Again, I felt my pulse quicken. *Calm down, Jeanne, calm down.*

'Well, of course, if you think I could help – if I won't be in the way . . .'

He was already striding towards the blue Peugeot with his phone pressed to his ear.

'Wait for me,' I called, running after him across the boulevard.

He stopped, put the phone to his chest. 'Do you know a winery called Château Lacasse, in Les Eglisottes?'

'No, I've never heard of it.'

'Good. Come on then, let's go.'

In less than half an hour we'd crossed the bridge that spans the sparkling waters of the Dordogne and were cruising along the four-lane Transeuropéenne highway past the town of Libourne. Lefèvre drove too fast. I glanced at the speedometer but had to look away when the needle skipped past one-forty – speeding is another of my pet hates. Even though he was a skilful driver, I was scared.

We came off the *autoroute* at Saint-Médart with the sun behind us. Long shadows, cast by the road signs, stretched across the exit road. Summer had passed so quickly. We crossed the River Isle, leaving behind the vineyards of the Libournais, and turned onto a narrow wooded lane. My heart rate settled, the gloom of dusk replaced the sunshine, and my mood darkened too.

I know what I'm like, what my *condition* is. It has a name, of course, but I don't like to use it and refuse to let it define me. Here's a clue: *when she was good, she was very good indeed, but when she was bad she was horrid.* Well, I've been like that ever since I was a little girl. They used

7

to say it was manic depression, but nowadays even French psychiatrists call it *bipolaire*.

Anyway, the lithium tablets never agreed with me, and I stopped taking them years ago. Since then, as long as I keep a check on my flights of fancy and surround myself with those I love – especially when the black thoughts threaten to strike – I get along just fine. And after the fairly manic series of events in 2009 that led to my getting shot, I'd managed to stay away from anything, well, too exciting. Until then, that is; until the phone call that put paid to my romantic evening with the captain. The grape harvest was almost upon me, I'd been elected to join the Jurade – the hallowed Saint-Emilion brotherhood – and now I was racing towards the scene of ... what? A suicide? A murder? Oh well, I said to myself, just remember two things Jeanne: remain calm and keep smiling.

I was still forcing a smile when I began to wonder if Lefèvre had taken a wrong turn. I've always trusted policemen, but I was starting to suspect that this one had no idea where the hell he was going.

'Do you know this area,' I asked, peering out at the dark forest.

He slowed to navigate a crossroads.

'Er, yes, yes I do. My father used to fish here when I was a boy, and then when I was about fifteen or sixteen we would camp here near the lake, you know – friends from school.'

I pictured the captain as a boy scout. It wasn't difficult.

'I never knew there was such a wilderness right on our doorstep.'

'Yes, it is quite remote. These woods are part of the great forest of Le Double – hundreds of square kilometres of trees that go from here right across the Perigord. Good hunting, too – wild boar, roe deer, some muntjac.'

My thoughts turned to the captain dressed in huntin',

shootin' and fishin' gear – a not unpleasant mental image. 'So, you're a keen hunter then?'

'What do you think?' he said, smiling. 'No, I read it in *La Chasse* in the dentist's waiting room.'

He took his phone from an inside pocket, flipped it open and pressed a couple of buttons.

'Okay, Jonzac, I'm in the woods a kilometre-or-so past the junction . . . On the left or the right? . . . Fine.'

Click.

He looked across at me. 'But it's not all trees; there is one huge vineyard in this section. Ah, here it is.'

The car slowed. There, on a rough verge, was a small hand-painted sign:

PROPRIÉTÉ PRIVÉE – DÉFENSE DE PÉNÉTRER

Keep out – not the usual advertisement that wineries put up to entice the passing trade.

We drove through the open gates, followed a winding, potholed drive, and there before us was the château, silhouetted against the orange glow of the western sky. With all its lights ablaze, the house resembled an enormous Halloween lantern. The windows in the tops of the two towers glowered at us threateningly; below them a row of stone mullions on the ground floor formed a malevolent scowl. If houses could speak, this one was saying: *turn round and go home.* Had I been on my own I'd have done just that because, although I was curious about the owner's demise, I was far from prepared for what we were about to discover.

Lefèvre parked between a couple of *Police Nationale* vehicles: a Traffic and a 308. There were several other cars on the drive including an expensive Mercedes, plus a Libourne ambulance. The registration plate on the back of the Merc, illuminated by the squad car's flashing blue light, bore a curious logo of a fork-bearing devil.

I could see quite a crowd assembled indoors, and the

lights were on in the winery too, but first we visited the house. I followed the captain up a half flight of stone steps and went inside. In the hallway a uniformed officer was taking notes from a fair-haired man of about my age. A pair of pale blue eyes glanced at me briefly before the man's attention returned the policeman. He muttered something, shook his head slowly and exhaled a loud sigh.

In the centre of the room a huddle of people, their expressions mirroring each other's concern, were talking in hushed, anxious tones. Lefèvre joined them, shook hands and listened solemnly to the information he was offered. The fair-haired man was escorted past me to the front door and he and the policeman exited the house.

I took in my surroundings. The room, which must once have been a grand entrance hall, was now almost empty of furniture or ornament. The windows needed cleaning; dusty cobwebs festooned the high ceiling's baroque mouldings; empty milk cartons and takeaway pizza boxes spilled from a collection of black bin bags; grimy terracotta tiles felt sticky underfoot.

I wandered through an open door and into a small study. On a leather-topped desk there sat a computer screen and a small stack of paperwork in neat-and-tidy contrast to the grubby disarray outside. The room contrasted, too, with my own study where groaning filing cabinets, sagging shelves and all untrod areas of floor space were home to an ever increasing deluge of paperwork. Apart from the desk, the screen and a tall louvered cabinet standing against the back wall, this office was bare.

'Come on, Jeanne, we need you in the vat house.'

The captain appeared in the doorway, glanced at the sparse contents of the little room and disappeared again. I hurried after him and we went outside, watched by the nervous delegation of officials in the hallway.

'Madame Coleville – the village mayor,' he explained, as we wove our way through the parked cars towards the winery buildings, 'her deputies and her secretary from the town hall, a journalist from *Le Sud Ouest*, the doctor of the deceased and a few others. Luckily not too many of them have—'

He stopped talking as we ducked under the cordon tape blocking the open door to the winery. The winemaker in me couldn't help feeling a pang of jealousy when I gazed at the rows of shiny stainless steel vats known as cuves, the heat exchangers and other pristine items of expensive equipment – couldn't help it, that is, until I looked up at the rim of the furthest vat. A red liquid appeared to have burst forth from the vat's top hatch, spilled down its polished steel sides and congealed there in long, russet-coloured rivulets; it didn't look like wine.

'*Mon dieu*, I wish Lieutenant Dauzac was here,' Lefèvre muttered.

We walked to the far end of the winery where we were greeted by two men wearing white body suits and another man – younger than the captain but dressed, like him, for an evening out – who was introduced to me as Docteur François Wissant, the pathologist.

'Got yourself a new lieutenant then, Lefèvre?' the man said, turning his smile on me.

'You know perfectly well he's on vacation, Wissant. This is Madame Valeix – she has offered to advise us on the . . . retrieval.'

I had no idea what he meant.

'Ah, yes. You've been briefed by the locals then? It's full to the brim, you know.'

'Yes, François. Two questions: how and how long ago?'

'A single, clean cut to the throat. Looks like it goes right through the carotid, jugular and windpipe. We think he was still alive when he was taken up there because there's not much blood on the steps. He could have been held over the open lid while his throat was slit. As for the time of death, I can't tell you yet – perhaps a week.'

'May I?' the captain said, pointing at the high walkway that ran the length of the winery, just above the tops of the vats. The white-suited men, who were collecting fibres from the steps of this metal scaffold, moved aside to let him pass.

Wissant tossed him a pair of latex gloves. 'Be my guest, Pierre, but put these on and try not to touch anything you shouldn't.' He turned to me and added, 'Perhaps you should move back a little, *madame*, in case any-thing . . . falls.'

I took two steps back and watched the captain climb the scaffold and open the vat's metal lid. His expression barely changed, but he recoiled at the sight of whatever floated on the surface of the vat's contents. He lowered the lid carefully and a putrid aroma, the like of which I've never smelled in any winery, preceded him as he climbed back down.

'Not a bad job, eh?' Wissant said, stony-faced.

'*Putain de merde*. The poor bastard.'

The men stood there silently, staring up at the lid of the vat, as though waiting for the stench to go away.

'Why you, Pierre? Why not the local *gendarmes*?'

'What, you mean apart from the fact that it's still the holidays and everyone is away?' He released his grip on the metal banister and folded his arms. 'No, they think there might be a drugs connection. It's such a professional job.'

'And is it?'

'Do you mean is it drugs related or a professional hit?'

'Either.'

'I don't know,' Lefèvre said quietly, 'I've never seen anything like it. It's so medieval.'

Wissant sighed. 'Murder's murder, my friend. Murder is murder. But whoever did this certainly knew what he was doing.'

Not for the first time that evening, I wondered why I was there; Lefèvre had the answer.

'Ah, yes, Jeanne. It seems that our friends next door would like Monsieur Rougeard – the dead man in this tank

– to be tucked up safely in the morgue before bedtime. But – and in this respect I must agree with my colleague here – we cannot just pluck him out like a goldfish from a bowl. It would be the devil of a job, and these men would get their lovely white clothes dirty. And I do not want any accidents. What we would like to do is drain the vat, collect a sample of the . . . liquid, and then retrieve Monsieur via this little door here.' He finished by indicating the small portal at the base of the cuve.

'How big is he?' I asked.

'We are told Monsieur Rougeard was a slight man, and what I have just seen confirms it.'

'Then I imagine he'll fit through the hatch.'

'Good, good,' Lefèvre said, gently leading me back towards the door. 'And you can drain the tank so we can open it? You will not be obliged to . . . see anything, believe me.'

I nodded.

'Okay, shall we get a breath of fresh air first?'

Leaning against the side panel of the Renault Traffic were two uniformed guards. They whispered to each other like naughty schoolboys, suppressed laughter punctuating their private conversation as they puffed on their cigarettes. As we approached I caught a few words and understood the source of their mirth.

'Oh, my God, yes. It'll have lots of body, that's for sure.'

'*Ah, oui,* imagine the health warning on the label: this product may contain traces of the winemaker—'

They noticed us and both stood to attention.

'*Bonsoir, Capitaine,*' they said in unison, almost poker-faced.

Lefèvre introduced me. '*Messieurs,* this is Madame Valeix, our expert witness.' The younger man was desperately trying not to laugh. 'In order to remove the body we need to empty the wine into the drain. She will show you how.'

The older of the two policemen furrowed his brow in mock concern. 'But chief, that's such a waste. Couldn't we save it for the brigade Christmas banquet?'

The young guard looked like he was about to burst.

Lefèvre ignored the leg-pull. 'Madame Valeix, how much wine is in that vat?'

I didn't need to think about it. 'Sixty-three *hectos* – about eight thousand bottles.'

Lefèvre made a calculation in his head, silently mouthing the sum, before addressing his subordinates. 'A coffee spoon, *messieurs*,' he said.

'What?' the older man asked.

'Monsieur Rougeard bled to death in that vat of wine. In his final moments he endured a most terrifying experience. So, that *wine*, boys, contains at least six litres of blood plus several other bodily fluids and waste products. Now, speaking as a detective, I would say that for every bottle of wine in there, you have about a coffee spoon of blood, piss and faeces mixed in. Would you really want to drink it?'

The men nodded. The younger one grimaced.

'Sorry about that Jeanne,' said Lefèvre. '*L'humour macabre*. It is what keeps us sane.'

We went back inside, and I asked the guards to fetch a wide-bore hose from the opposite end of the vat house. They ambled off, still talking in lowered voices. 'I think I've tasted wine like that,' said one. '*Ah, oui,* they serve it in the station canteen,' said the other.

'Quickly!' Lefèvre called to them, 'we don't have all night.' He sighed as we watched them fumbling with the tubing. 'Nearly fifteen years of service but only four stripes between them. Good men though.'

'I'm impressed with your mental arithmetic, *Capitaine*.'

'What, the coffee spoon? I just made it up. Go on, show them what to do, then we might go and have a quick chat with the neighbour before I take you home.'

After emptying the vat, I was invited to go and wait in the house. I don't know why, but I asked if I could stay. It wasn't that I wanted to see the body, particularly; I just had to remain connected with the events. Or perhaps I was simply drawn to the captain, reluctant to leave him. In the end they allowed me to stand by the open door, several metres away from the action.

Apart from the time I glimpsed my own mortality at the wrong end of a gun, I've witnessed death three times in my life. I've buried three men. Three men whom I loved, in different ways, and still mourn: my young husband, Olivier, who was killed in a road accident delivering his Saint-Emilion wine; his father, Henri, who died of a broken heart; and my mid-life love, Andrew, whose extended stay at the vineyard changed my life forever and marked the final chapter of his. Three times bereaved and twice widowed, I'm familiar with death, you see; so the blood-stained cuve in Rougeard's winery held no fears for me.

Or so I thought.

Monsieur Rougeard – his hands tied in front, a black, gaping gash across his neck that went from one ear to the other – lay in a pool of blood and wasted wine on the tiled floor. The most striking thing about the body wasn't the slashed throat, nor the puffy, decomposing features, nor the eyes which, even from a distance, I could see protruding like those of a poached fish. No, the most obvious thing about Monsieur Rougeard's corpse was its colour. Every square inch of exposed skin, from his bald head to his bare forearms, bound wrists and hands, was stained a dark shade of crimson. After marinating for God-knows how long in a vat of Bordeaux wine, Monsieur Rougeard had turned red.

When the smell – and the rising feeling of sickening horror in my stomach – became unbearable I fled from the vat-house, thankful I hadn't eaten anything that evening.

To get to the neighbour's house entailed a five minute

drive – left on the forest road, then another left into a newly laid gravel courtyard. Unlike Rougeard's place, Domaine du Soleil had a colourful sign advertising wine tastings and guided tours. I noticed the sign's paintwork which, though clean and new, was bordered by what looked like strips of adhesive tape and torn paper.

Parked in the middle of the courtyard was a shiny new Range Rover. The glow from a porch light, that came on as we approached, glinted on the vehicle's burgundy paintwork. The registration plates were French, but the steering wheel, I noticed, was on the right.

The front door was opened by the fair-haired man I'd seen earlier. Even before he spoke, I knew he was English.

'*Bonsoir*,' he said, glancing over his shoulder when a loud crash resounded in the entrance hall. 'Sorry, it's the dogs. Please, come in.'

The sound of whining, sniffing and scratching came from behind a door I hoped was securely closed.

'Good evening, *monsieur. Captaine Pierre Lefèvre, Police Nationale.*'

'Oh, good evening.'

'And this is Madame Valeix. She is assisting us because, like Monsieur Rougeard, she is a winemaker.'

'As I am too, *monsieur*,' the man said. 'A winemaker, I mean.'

'Yes, of course. And, like you, she is also English.'

We shook hands. 'John Clare,' he said. He was smartly dressed, not tall but not short either. His friendly face wore an exasperated expression.

'Jeanne, Jeanne Valeix.'

'The kettle's just boiled. Would you like some tea?'

I wanted to ask for something stronger but accepted his offer politely. We followed him into a large kitchen which, like the entrance hall, was decorated with impeccable taste and flamboyant style; an expensive renovation, no doubt.

Lefèvre was clearly impressed. 'You have a beautiful home, Monsieur Clare.'

'Thank you, Captain. Yes, it was hard work to get it like this, though. The kitchen was being used as a piggery when we bought the place.'

The policeman ran his hand along the zinc counter top. 'We?'

'Yes. My partner and I. But I live alone now – please do sit down.'

We sat at an oak refectory table while Clare busied himself with making the tea.

After passing us our cups he said, 'I still just can't believe it.'

'What can't you believe, *monsieur*?'

Clare sat down. He stared at the captain, taking shallow breaths, then took a sip of tea. 'I'm not – *was* not – a friend of Rougeard's. Everyone knows that. Even before we came here, before we'd signed the papers, divided the vineyard, I knew he was going to be trouble. But Ash was struck on this place—'

'Your partner?' Lefèvre interrupted.

'Yes. Anyway, from day one Rougeard was trouble. We never got on, and I can't think of a single person round here who liked him any more than I did. But I can't imagine anyone doing *that*.'

He nodded in the vague direction of his neighbour's property, raised his teacup with a trembling hand, then put it back down again.

'Monsieur Clare, would you tell me exactly how you discovered the body of Monsieur Rougeard?'

'I . . .' he began, then turned to me. 'Look, I'm sorry, but why are you here? I mean, he speaks English, so—'

'As I said, Madame Valeix is a winemaker like you. She is helping us with the technical details. If you would prefer that she wait outside?'

'No, of course not. I'm sorry, my nerves are a bit frayed.'

'I know what you mean,' I said, gently touching the man's sleeve. I wasn't lying.

'No, honestly, you have no idea.' He sipped his tea,

17

shifted in his chair. 'So, where are your vines then, Madame . . . ?'

'Please, call me *Jeanne*.'

He smiled.

'Jeanne.'

'I have a vineyard in Saint-Emilion.'

'Wow, I'm impressed. How many hectares? Have you got a vat house like Rougeard's?'

I drained my cup. 'Only four, and, no, my winery is far more modest.'

'Mine too. I was amazed when I saw all the kit he'd got. I'd heard about it, but until this afternoon I hadn't been into the winery since we moved here.'

'So why the visit today, *monsieur*?' asked Lefèvre.

'We start the harvest next week. I imagine you're busy preparing too aren't you, Jeanne? Got your team lined up?'

'I'm trying to organise everything,' I said, 'looks like we'll start around the 10th.'

'Me too.' He turned to Lefèvre. 'In previous years a team of grape pickers has harvested my crop as well as Rougeard's. This year no one has heard from him, and as his vines cover about twelve hectares and I only have two, there's a chance the grape pickers might let me down – you know, take on a bigger contract. So I drove over there this afternoon—'

'At what time?' Lefèvre cut in.

'At six o'clock – the traffic news had just come on the radio.'

I looked at Clare. He seemed reluctant to relate the rest of the tale.

'And when you arrived at the home of Monsieur Rougeard?' Lefèvre prompted.

'When I got to the château his Mercedes was there on the drive and the door to the winery was open. I expected him to appear as soon as I pulled up. He didn't, so I went inside. I noticed the blood . . . climbed up to the top of the vat . . . opened the hatch . . .'

18

He stood up and took his cup over to the sink. When he turned round his face was ashen.

'He . . . bobbed up – that's the only way I can describe it. You know, not floated up, he bobbed up out of the wine. His head and shoulders came up out of the hatch for Christ's sake! I slammed the lid down and felt it bump the top of his head – Jesus the *smell*.'

He looked down at his hands which, though linked together, were still trembling.

'And the colour of his skin! The *colour!*'

'Thank you, *monsieur*,' Lefèvre said, standing up. 'You get some rest now. Tomorrow I may return if that will not inconvenience you?'

'No, not at all. I have no plans. I'll be here all day.'

'Goodnight then, Monsieur Clare.'

I said goodnight too, adding, 'John, if your pickers do let you down then my team might be interested. They usually go up to the Charente after picking my vines, but maybe they could come here before going north.'

'Thank you. Yes, that's good to know. I don't know what I'm going to do otherwise.'

'I'll telephone tomorrow – they're a motley bunch but they do a good job.'

'Thank you,' he said again.

We didn't talk much on the way back to my place. Lefèvre seemed preoccupied with his thoughts. Once we were out of the woods he opened a CD and slipped the disk into the car's stereo. Joni Mitchell's lilting soprano drifted though the dark space between us.

> *You're in my blood, you're like holy wine,*
> *You taste so bitter, taste so sweet,*
> *Oh, I could drink a case of you,*
> *And still be on my feet.*

I'd read somewhere – but never really understood – that murder is an aphrodisiac, that the unconscious mind, when confronted with sudden or violent death, can go into procreational overdrive. Well, it hadn't been a romantic night; might there still be time for the mood to change? I listened to the song's lyrics and, despite the horrors I'd encountered at Lacasse, began to fantasise about how the evening might end – the tentative kiss, the invitation to stay, the adrenal rush of excitement. I looked at the man's rugged features and thought: I could drink a case of you, Lefèvre, though I'm not sure I'd still be on my feet . . . Well, one day maybe but, no, not tonight; there were too many people at home, for one thing.

We skirted Saint-Emilion with the lights from the village visible on the high côte to our left and arrived at Château Fontloube, my home. Lefèvre slowed as we passed between the stone gateposts, then pulled up on the gravel drive in front of the house. He yanked the handbrake, and for a moment we sat there silently, gazing at the wisteria-clad limestone facade. Despite being draughty and cold in winter, stuffy in summer, blissfully free of most modern conveniences, and a sinkhole for my hard-earned euros, Fontloube still warms my heart whenever I return home. Even after spending half my life here, I never tire of its timeless charm. The windows in the upstairs gallery were dark, as were the mansards in the roof and those in the two *tourelle* towers. The only light emanated from the kitchen to the side of the house.

'I'm sorry,' he said.

'What for – tonight or the other thing?'

'Both. Look Jeanne, we did everything we could back in March you know.'

'Yes, I know. And at least he's in prison. But only *ten years*, Pierre?'

'The murder charge was never going to stick, not with the lack of evidence. But do not worry, Popescu is locked away in La Santé, and when he gets out we should be able to have him deported. Anyway, you will never have to be involved in all that stuff again.'

Bad memories, like murderers, are best kept locked

away. But sometimes they escape. Six months had gone by since the trial, but suddenly I was there again, in the courtroom, fascinated and horrified by the cold indifference of the man in the dock – the man who killed Aimée Loroux.

A tear settled on my lower eyelid and I tried desperately to blink it away, not wanting the captain to see me cry. He opened the door an inch and the car filled with a yellow light. The tear trickled down my cheek and soaked into the seatbelt. When he looked at me I embraced him, resting my head on the padded shoulder of his jacket.

'How is it that a man like Popescu can get away with murder?' I sobbed.

We sat there for a moment, staring through the windscreen at a flight of bats. Dark shadows, cast by the headlights' glare, fluttered across the pale-golden stonework of the house.

'I am not an expert on the justice system, Jeanne. I am just a policeman. You win some, you lose some. You just have to try to make sure the next one doesn't get away with it.'

I dabbed my eyes with a handkerchief and then looked at my date. 'You think you can catch whoever murdered Rougeard, then?'

Lefèvre's frown said it before he did.

'*Qui sait.*'

Something about his reply reminded me of a question I'd wanted to ask earlier that evening. 'By the way, how did you know about the Jurade?'

His gaze drifted from my face to the moonlit vines.

'Oh, you know,' he said, sniffing, 'on the . . . vine grape, *c'est ça?*'

'You mean *grapevine*.'

'Grapevine,' he repeated slowly. 'Yes, and I also know who proposed you.'

'Well?'

'Commissaire Lamarque, the chief superintendent.'

I'd had doubts, of course, about Saint-Emilion's

secret society, the Jurade. I've never been much of a joiner, always held Wilde's view that any club that would accept me could not be worth joining. Still, I do enjoy dressing up, and it would be good for business after all. But now, it seemed, news of my forthcoming investiture had passed through the ranks of Libourne's police department. So much for secrecy.

'Really,' I said, 'and how's your boss connected with the Jurade?'

'Oh, he's a member of the inner council. I think *le marguillier* is his ceremonial title. You know how it is – married into one of Saint-Emilion's prominent wine families. Old money and old wine. And he's a director of the château.'

I was curious. 'Which one?'

He told me; I was impressed.

'Anyway,' I said. 'I'm not sure I'll be accepting the invitation. I don't like clubs.'

'Jeanne,' he said, leaning closer, 'day after day it seems as though the bad guys get away with murder. But sometimes, just sometimes, the good guys get rewarded. You are one of the good guys, Jeanne. Accept it.'

He kissed me.

It was a small, ambiguous kiss, but I accepted it – gladly; I was just trying to work out whether it was intended as a polite gesture of farewell or something more amorous when my friend, Wendy, appeared at the side door of the house, her bulky frame silhouetted by the kitchen's florescent light.

'There is an old woman watching us,' Lefèvre whispered.

Wendy Snook, my septuagenarian houseguest, dressed in a silk dressing gown and my wellington boots, waved at us vigorously. A second later a Jack Russell terrier's muzzle appeared in the gap in the open driver's door. Lefèvre opened the door a little wider and my dog, Turk, introduced himself with a friendly bark.

'Don't mind old Turk,' I said, unfastening my

seatbelt, 'he likes policemen.'

I stepped out into the warm night and then ducked down to say goodbye.

'So he should,' Lefèvre said, 'we are good guys too, you know.'

'Goodnight, Captain Lefèvre.'

'Goodnight, Madame Valeix.'

I ambled towards the house, with Turk trotting ahead, then turned round to wave goodbye and watch Lefèvre's tail-lights disappear at the end of the drive.

'It's so late, my gorgeous girl, we were worried about you.' Wendy's familiar lisp indicated that her dentures were, by now, soaking in Steradent for the night. 'The young people have already gone to bed. How was your evening?'

I turned back to the house. 'I've had better.'

'Oh, I'm sorry, dear. I hope I didn't—'

'No, Wendy, don't worry.'

As I approached the open door to the kitchen, I could tell from her sparkly-eyed expression and toothless grin that Wendy was dying to know every detail of my date with Lefèvre.

We went indoors. 'Well, it's obvious he likes you, Jeanne,' Wendy said.

'What makes you say that?' I asked, closing the kitchen door behind me.

'There's no question about it! Did you see the look he gave you when you said goodnight?'

'What look?'

'*That* look. The face that men pull when they're interested.' She opened the cupboard, and I heard the chink of glasses. 'It's the same look a puppy dog gives you—' She put two brandy glasses on the kitchen table, and we both sat down. '—usually five minutes before he does his business on your best rug.'

In spite of the awfulness of the evening's main event, I couldn't help laughing.

23

'Oh, I'm sure the captain is fully housetrained, Wendy.'

'Yes, indeed, my gorgeous. I imagine he is.' She poured two generous shots of cognac. 'So, how did it go?'

I prepared myself for a thorough cross-examination. 'It's a long story, Wendy.'

Wendy, as well as being a retired academic, is an avid collector of gossip – an essential character trait, she says, for a historian – and she has a fiendish, curious mind. Miss Marple, we call her. In looks, too, she is remarkably similar to Dame Rutherford's matronly detective. Cruelly, I told her as much once. She replied that I looked like a young Jacqueline Bisset; if only I could have rewound my words. We've been the best of friends ever since, and she's a welcome and frequent visitor to Fontloube.

'Oh, but you're crying, my dear,' she said, clasping my hands in hers. 'What on earth happened?'

'Wendy,' I said, sniffing, 'you won't believe what I saw tonight.'

That night, before turning off the lamp, I scribbled the words *la rentrée* on a piece of paper and propped it next to my alarm clock.

I dreamed that my grape pickers had deserted me, and I had to bring in the entire crop on my own. The temperature on the vineyard thermometer was rising to 40 degrees Celsius, and the fruit was rapidly rotting on the vines. I gathered what I could, the bunches deliquescing in my hands, the juice running through my dark-stained fingers onto the stony ground. I worked all day until the vats were full, but the juice had turned to blood, the crop was spoiled, a whole year's work wasted, flushed down the drain.

Lundi 5 Séptembre 2011

The alarm clock on my bedside table buzzed. I reached over to turn the damn thing off, and there on the clock face was my hand-written note to remind me that this was the start of the autumn term, the beginning of the new school year.

I leapt out of bed feeling unusually energised despite yesterday's late night and bedtime brandies. While brushing my teeth, my stomach gurgled as loudly as the antiquated water pipes in the bathroom, and I understood the cause of my get-up-and-go mood: I hadn't eaten for eighteen hours. Thoughts turned therefore to breakfast and focussed on the buttery croissants, crisp on the outside and light but doughy in the middle, awaiting me at the village bakery.

I showered quickly, changed into a light calico dress and slipped my feet into a pair of sandals. It was only seven a.m. but the air, barely stirring the curtains at the open window, was already warm. The forecasters had predicted a hot, dry September – just the kind of weather I needed to harvest my ripening grapes. But this day threatened to be a stormy one.

Parking my anxieties about the weather and the harvest for the time being, I jogged downstairs, grabbed my car keys and went outside into the sunshine.

After touching, for luck, the silver Saint Christopher that covers a bullet hole in Clementine's dashboard, I drove up the vineyard track towards the village. My bright orange Citroën 2CV suffers from countless mechanical ailments, among them faulty wipers, a leaky roof, doors that either can't be locked or refuse to open, usually when it's raining. But I love her dearly.

When I reached the crest of the côte, there, spread out before me, was the verdant plain of the Dordogne, a million vines bearing a billion grapes ripening in the morning sun. On the northern horizon a rainbow emerged from a low bank of dark cloud. It was raining on someone's vineyard.

After over twenty years living here in France I have never grown tired of the daily journey to the *boulangerie* – or the taste of warm croissants for breakfast.

Twenty minutes later I was back at Fontloube bearing a paper sack of patisseries and a couple of baguettes. The smell of fresh coffee drifted from the kitchen, and there I found Archie, my talented student oenologist, diligently setting the table.

'Morning, Jeanne,' he muttered, his dreamy-blue eyes fluttering as he continued to arrange the crockery and cutlery just-so.

'Good morning, Archie,' I replied. 'All set for college?'

His eyelids flickered again but his attention stayed focussed on the breakfast things.

'S'pose.'

Archie Maconie, Andrew's son, came to Fontloube after his father passed away. Adopting him and making him a business partner were decisions I have never regretted. He's the apple of my eye and the closest thing I have to a family. He's also often quite undemonstrative. But this response was unusually terse, even for him. He could appear downright rude at times, but I'd long since stopped taking offense. Archie has Asperger's Syndrome. Not that it has held him back in any way; apart from being a tad uncommunicative, he has a lightning-sharp memory, an uncanny ability to calculate and catalogue, and a talent for languages. For a twenty-one-year-old with autism he does pretty well. And he also has a very rare form of synaesthesia that allows him – no, *forces* him – to 'see' smells. He's a natural-born winemaker and will, one day I'm sure, be one of Bordeaux's top oenologists.

When my other student resident breezed into the room I guessed the cause of Archie's introspective mood: he might not know it yet but the boy was clearly in love.

'*Bonjour,* Jeanne. *Bonjour,* Archie.'

Archie's face lit up.

Nearly a week had passed since Loubna Ben Moumen's arrival, but I was still unaccustomed to the Moroccan girl's stunning beauty. She wore her hair long, its luscious dark curls falling to her shoulders from under a loose-fitting *hijab*. Her features had retained a child-like softness but her emerald eyes burned with a passion quite at odds with her natural shyness. A trace of the guttural consonants of her mother tongue gave her French voice an exotic, sensual nuance. She was raised in the foothills of the Atlas Mountains and, at twenty, had the charm, strength and intelligence of a Brontë heroine. Not surprisingly, Archie worshipped her.

'*Bonjour, Loubna. Bien dormi?*' I asked.

Yes, she told me, as Archie pulled out a chair for her, she had slept very well. I shook out the patisserie into a bread basket, and she had just begun to tell me how excited she was to be going to a French university when my third houseguest entered the kitchen and flashed us all a smile – thankfully a toothy one.

'*Bonjour,* my dears!' Wendy warbled. 'Ah, croissants!'

Loubna and I said good morning; Archie remained silent.

Wendy gave the boy a sidelong glance and reached for the teapot. 'Loubna,' she said, 'you are quite simply the most exquisite, gorgeous girl I have ever set eyes on.'

Archie tapped his butter knife nervously on the side of his plate and blushed.

His thoughts had been voiced.

After breakfast, I drove my young apprentices to the Faculty of Oenology in Libourne. Archie would be starting the second year of his degree, and Loubna was enrolling there as an overseas student on a foreign exchange programme. As the only child of a successful Moroccan *vigneron*, she was spending a year in Saint-Emilion to learn how to grow vines and make wine the French way. Luckily, her father didn't mind that she would be learning most of the practical stuff from me – an Englishwoman. Apparently he hoped she'd improve her English, too.

I dropped the two of them off at the college and followed the one-way system along the Cours Tourny. At the junction near the pizza restaurant a police car cut in front of me and hared off with its blue lights flashing. At the next block, there it was again, parked in front of the *hôtel de police*. The traffic slowed and stopped, and I glanced at the occupants of the car. Two disinterested-looking police officers sat in the back flanking a small, dark-skinned man with a shaved head. His lip was swollen and he held a white gauze pad to his forehead. Just when the cars in front started to move again he looked at me. His face bore a fearful, piteous expression.

Back at Fontloube, I found a note Wendy had scribbled on the back of an unused wine label saying that she was taking a bath and then taking me to lunch. Lunch sounded like a great idea, but first I had a couple of items to tick off my to-do list. I took the refractometer into the vineyard to check on the fruit's sugar levels. The gadget told me the grapes were almost ripe, but Turk hadn't started eating them yet – a sure sign the fruit was not quite ready. This year Mother Nature would bring an early harvest, probably starting at the weekend, and so I needed to make sure my team of grape pickers would be there.

I stashed the gadget in the leather satchel, then went back to the study to telephone the itinerant vineyard workers who come to Fontloube year after year. We would start the merlot harvest on the 11th of September and, if all went well, finish the cabernets by the 15th. After that, my team would go up to John Clare's place and bring in his couple of hectares before moving on again.

Wendy and I couldn't agree on who would buy lunch; she wanted to repay my hospitality, and I – well, I just didn't want her to pay. In the end we settled on an agreeable compromise: we'd go to an expensive restaurant and split the bill fifty-fifty. Since it was a Monday, and most of the local places would be closed, we'd need to drive into the city to find a good restaurant. Luckily, I knew just the place.

Chez Stéphane is, as far as I'm concerned, the best restaurant in Bordeaux. The fact that the chef-patron, Stéphane Lavergne, is a close friend of mine is almost irrelevant. He now has a Michelin star to praise his superlative cuisine and a brigade of wannabe master chefs under his command. And he serves my wine, Château Fontloube, which proves he's as discerning in the cellar as he is talented in the kitchen.

I was looking forward to seeing him again and hoped that a certain young apprentice of his would be there too. Valentin Valeix, my late husband's second cousin, had worked for me in the past, but he'd decided to follow his dream to become a top chef. Now he was working for Stéphane, and I was dying to know how the boy was getting along.

We found a parking place beneath a shady plane tree on the Place des Grands Hommes, and went the rest of the way on foot. The air, heavy with the threat of a thunderstorm, smelled of coffee, tar and diesel fumes mixed with the occasional whiff of drains and the ever-present aroma of the quaysides. Bordeaux's smell, on such a hot day, is as foreign and exotic to me now as it was when I first came. Wendy struggled wheezily along the pavement. Chez Stéphane's bright, air-conditioned dining room was a welcome relief from the muggy heat outside.

The dozen-or-so diners, mostly businesspeople, barely noticed us as we followed a slender young waiter to our table. Wendy wasted no time in requesting an aperitif, and the waiter scuttled off to summon the sommelier.

A few seconds later I spotted Valentin strolling confidently towards us. He wore a starched white shirt and black waistcoat complete with a shiny silver *tastevin* dangling from a chain round his neck. So smart, I thought, so grown up. He'd been a cocky teenager with holes in his jeans when he first came to Fontloube. So much had changed since that unforgettable summer; was it only three years ago?

He embraced us both, first Wendy, then me.

'Look at you, all dressed up,' I said, 'shouldn't you be in chef's whites?'

'All part of the training, Jeanne. Monsieur Lavergne thinks I'll make a good wine waiter.'

'If you can sell wine to this lot,' I said, eyeing the clientele, 'as well as you did at Fontloube, then I'm sure Monsieur Lavergne will be very pleased with you.'

He went to fetch our drinks, returning a few moments later with a couple of glasses of ice-cold crémant and a small dish of tasty amuse-bouches.

We toasted each other's health, ordered the fixed *menu d'affaire*, and I asked Valentin if he could suggest the wine.

'I will bring you something suitable,' he said.

'Oh, well done, gorgeous boy,' Wendy said. 'I hate decisions. No lady ever cheerfully chose a claret!'

We nibbled the appetisers, sipped our fizz, and Wendy began to tell me about a recent lunch she'd had with a colleague. Valentin reappeared, proudly displaying the bottle he'd selected. I recognised the label; it was one of the restaurant's cheaper wines.

Wendy grimaced.

'I'm sorry, *madame*,' he said. 'You don't like this wine?'

'On the contrary, dear boy, I keep a little in my own cellar. I serve it to hasten the departure of lingering houseguests.'

Valentin looked at me, nonplussed.

'Perhaps you could fetch us a bottle of Fontloube?' I suggested. 'I think you still have the 2005?'

He went back to the cellar, returned with a bottle of my wine and began to uncork it at a small side table.

'It was a frightful lunch,' Wendy was saying. 'She's a devotee of one of those diets that proscribe all forms of carbohydrate – including alcohol!'

'That sounds terrible, Wendy.'

'Quite,' she said, staring at the back of Valentin's tight trousers while he extracted the cork. 'A meal without wine is such a flat affair, don't you agree?'

I nodded. Valentin poured me a taster as Wendy continued. 'It lacks the essential third dimension that a claret or a burgundy brings to the feast. A bottle of wine is the table's exclamation mark. It looks down on the plates and dishes, knives and forks that simply say "eat", and proclaims "drink and be merry!"'

Once I'd stopped giggling I sniffed my glass. 'Thank you, Valentin, it's fine.'

He filled our glasses, replaced the bottle on the side table and gave a small bow before turning to leave.

Wendy, smiling, clearly proud of her homespun bons mots, called to him in a sing-song voice: 'Valentin, did you know that before the war wine was routinely removed from the table?'

'Ah . . . no, *madame*.'

'Apparently,' she went on, 'in those days most wine was of very dubious provenance. It was removed to avoid any scrutiny of the label that might reveal what a sham the bottle contained.'

'I see,' the poor boy said.

'Now, as the authenticity of this wine is unquestionable, I'd like to keep it here on the table if it's all the same to you.'

He conveyed our bottle to the table with a polite '*Je vous en prie, madame*'.

'I promise to gaze at it adoringly, my dear,' she said, adding, *sotto voce*, 'and top up our glasses as and when I choose, eh, Jeanne?'

'Quite so, Wendy. Cheers!'

'Bottoms up!'

After a plate of pan-fried calf's liver with green peppercorn sauce followed by a perfect *fondant au chocolat*, we were enjoying our coffees in the company of *le patron*, Stéphane Lavergne. I asked him why Valentin had been allowed out of the kitchen. Apparently the boy was as keen to learn the front-of-house aspects of restauranting as he was the secrets of the kitchen. It was quite obvious, Stéphane told me, that Valentin had ambitions to run his own restaurant. Why was he so sure? When he was Valentin's age, he said, he'd been exactly the same – work in a top chef's kitchen, learn the ropes of the business, then take on the world.

'I'm sure Valentin won't let you down,' I said.

'As long as his achievements match his potential, he won't.'

I remembered Valentin's early experiments in the kitchen at Fontloube. 'He used to make very good pastry,' I said.

Stéphane looked left and right before leaning forward towards us. 'He has a great talent,' he said. 'The problem is that he is too . . . proud, too vain.'

'Ah, but mark the difference, dear boy,' Wendy interjected. 'Vanity is pride without substance, whereas pride is substance without vanity.'

Our host took in Wendy's wise words and nodded.

'He was telling us all about wine fraud,' she lied. 'He's incredibly knowledgeable.'

Stéphane's nodding stopped. 'What sort of wine fraud?' he asked.

'Oh, you know,' she said, 'second-rate wine being

sold as top-class Bordeaux.'

'Ha! it goes on everywhere,' he said. 'The Yanks, the Brits, the Dutch . . . They will buy anything with the right label. Listen, this week I heard of a certain *grand cru classé* changing hands for only forty euros a bottle.'

I was curious. 'Which one?'

'Cheval Blanc 1990, apparently, but I don't believe it. The crooks forge the wine labels, stick them on the right kind of bottles which they fill with any old rubbish and, *voila*, a ten franc wine can be sold for a small fortune!'

Just then Valentin appeared.

'Ah, Valeix,' Stéphane said, slapping the boy on the back, 'so you are an expert on wine fraud now, eh?'

He looked at Wendy and, without his boss seeing, winked at her. 'No, Chef, not an expert. I was just telling Mesdames that before the war many wines were of very dubious . . . provenance.'

'There, you see Stéphane,' Wendy said, beaming at Valentin, 'so very, very knowledgeable.'

We took the scenic route back from Bordeaux. Wendy was on the passenger side of the bench seat next to me, snoring.

I glanced at my lucky Saint Christopher on the dashboard, remembering why it was there. Eighteen months before, a man called Grigor Popescu had come to Bordeaux from Bucharest, killed Aimée Loroux then shot me with a 9mm Beretta. The bullet grazed my neck and came to rest in Clémentine's wiper mechanism. Popescu was given a ten-year sentence for drugs trafficking but was acquitted of Aimée's murder. I still have a pale scar on my neck, and the car's wipers have never worked properly since. In fact, as we crossed the river at Branne, they were struggling to cope with the rainstorm that had finally caught up with us.

I was desperately peering through the rain-lashed windscreen when the phone rang. I pulled over, rummaged through my handbag and only just managed to find the thing before the ringing stopped.

It was Lefèvre.

'Jeanne, I need a favour.'

The sound of his voice took me back instantly to the kiss in the car. 'Of course, Captain. How can I help?'

'We have detained Monsieur Clare for questioning concerning René Rougeard's death. He is refusing to answer any questions without an English interpreter.'

Detained? I couldn't believe John Clare had anything to do with Rougeard's murder. 'I'm not sure I should be getting involved—'

'Look, Jeanne, we're really short staffed. I don't have anyone to interpret for him. He's asking for you.'

How could I refuse? 'Okay, Captain,' I said. 'But why have you brought him to Libourne?'

Wendy woke up and sat forward, staring at the deluge outside.

'He is . . . connected to a young Algerian who used to work for Rougeard – look, I will give you the details when you get here.'

I remembered the North African man in the car outside the *hôtel de police*. 'What do you mean *connected*?'

'I will explain everything when I see you, but Monsieur Clare is a . . . *homosexuel*.'

My God, I thought, you don't need to be a detective to work that one out. 'Yes, but—'

'Look, just get here as soon as you can. Please.'

Wendy offered to go with me to the police station, but I told her not to bother. I'd pop in to see Lefèvre, talk to John Clare and then collect Archie and Loubna from college. I didn't think it would take long.

When I arrived outside the *hôtel de police* I was amazed at the attention the Police Nationale were devoting to Lefèvre's investigation. All the parking bays on the block were taken by marked police vehicles, and a small army of uniformed officers were to-ing and fro-ing along the pavement, talking into mobile phones, and giving or receiving orders. I parked on the Place Surchamp, then walked to the station in the shade of the avenue's plane trees. The rain, it seemed, had stopped.

When I arrived the captain was standing on the steps at the front of the building. I couldn't help admiring his uniform: the pale blue short-sleeved shirt emblazoned with the tricolore and triple-striped epaulettes, the tight, dark navy trousers, the holstered gun at his belt, the shiny black rangers. He wasn't wearing the old-fashioned *képi* police cap, but you can't have everything I suppose. He looked, dare I say it, quite sexy. After finishing a conversation with one of the two officers I'd met the previous night he ushered me into the station. I followed him past the front desk to a stairway that descended into the basement.

On the way down, Lefèvre began to fill me in.

'We talked to the bar owner in Les Eglisottes. There was a fight there last week between Rougeard and an ex-employee of his. They were both arrested by the local *gendarmes*.'

At the end of a long, bright corridor we reached a pale green metal door. Lefèvre gripped the handle. 'Clare is a friend of the other man.' He opened the door and we entered the room. John Clare, a little weary-looking, was sitting behind a large Formica-topped table. He stood, scraping his chair as he did so, and put out his hand to me.

'Oh, Jeanne, thank you for coming.'

We shook hands. I told him it was no trouble.

The three of us sat down and Lefèvre started to explain why Clare was there. A week earlier, the owner of the Bar des Sports in Les Eglisottes had called the *gendarmes* when an argument between René Rougeard and his former employee, an Algerian called Hakim Wattar, had turned violent. Apparently Rougeard had accused Wattar of stealing from him; Wattar, it seemed, held a grudge against his ex-boss who owed him several weeks' wages. The two men were detained overnight in the *gendarmerie* and released the following day.

'So far, so straightforward,' Lefèvre said. 'But the disagreement between Rougeard and Wattar was more complex than that, was it not, Monsieur Clare?'

'Not really, no,' said Clare, leaning back with his arms folded, sighing loudly. 'Look, is this going to take much longer?'

'Please, be patient, Monsieur Clare. I am only trying to help Madame Valeix understand.'

I looked from one man to the other.

'When Rougeard fired Wattar, Monsieur Clare here helped the man financially – *n'est-ce pas, monsieur*?'

Clare turned to me. 'He had no job and nowhere to live. I lent him some money so he could put a deposit on a rented flat in the village and buy a scooter. He's paying me back by working at my place.'

'All very praiseworthy, Monsieur Clare. But Rougeard was making accusations against the two of you, yes?' Lefèvre went over to a small desk set against the wall and returned with a rolled-up piece of paper. 'This,' he said, unrolling what looked like a weather-worn poster, 'is the sort of thing Rougeard was saying about you.'

> *Leur vigne est du plant de Sodome*
> *Et du terroir de Gomorrhe*
> *Leurs raisins sont des raisins empoisonnés*
> *Leurs grappes sont amères*
> *Leur vin, c'est le venin des serpents*
> *C'est le poison cruel des aspics*

The biblical references to Sodom and Gomorrah and poisonous wine were fairly obvious, but how had they been levelled at John Clare? He explained: 'Rougeard stuck that to the sign at the end of my drive.'

'Oh, John,' I said, 'how horrible!'

Lefèvre, keen no doubt to ensure we both understood the text, gave us his translation. 'Their vine comes from the plant of Sodom and the fields of Gomorrah . . . their grapes are poisonous, their bunches are bitter, their wine is the venom of snakes . . . it is the cruel poison of . . .' He furrowed his brow, unable to translate the last word.

'Asps, perhaps?' I suggested.

'Yes, asps,' he concluded.

John was still looking at me. 'He thinks Hakim killed Rougeard, or maybe he thinks both of us did – there's no way Hakim is strong enough to . . . you know.'

'Perhaps, now that Madame Valeix is here, John, you could tell me exactly what happened between you and Wattar and Rougeard?'

Clare took a deep breath.

'Rougeard was a nasty piece of work, okay? As well as being a bully, a bigot and a religious nut, he exploited Hakim's weaknesses, kept him working there for next to nothing. Then when his business was nearly bankrupt, he kicked Hakim out. God knows how, but a few months later he was driving around in a brand new Mercedes and offering to buy back my land at more than I'd paid for it. When I refused he began this sort of . . . vendetta against me.'

'A vendetta, *monsieur*?'

'Well, a series of events, really. He deliberately damaged some trellising, then last spring he sprayed my vines with herbicide. He even tried to kill the dogs with rat poison. I reported it all to the local *gendarmes*, you can ask them.'

'I have done, Monsieur Clare. They also told me Rougeard had made several offensive remarks about you and Wattar' – he indicated the poster – 'and it was something of *this* nature that caused Hakim Wattar to assault Rougeard in the bar.'

Clare remained silent for a few seconds. 'Hakim is an alcoholic, but he is also a very religious man. If Rougeard started saying those ridiculous things in the bar then it must have upset him. But he's not a violent person.'

Lefèvre made a note in a small writing pad. 'You say "must have"? You have not seen Monsieur Wattar since the fight in the bar?'

Clare looked away. 'He phoned me the following morning to say he wouldn't be coming to the winery that day. I haven't seen him since.'

Lefèvre stood up, propping his weight on the table with two closed fists. 'Are you and Hakim Wattar engaged in a sexual relationship, Monsieur Clare?'

Clare looked shocked but kept his cool. 'No, we are not, and I don't see what that—'

'You are a homosexual, are you not, Monsieur Clare?'

'Nice friend you have here, Jeanne—'

'Just answer the question, please, *monsieur*.'

'Yes, I am. But the relationship between Hakim and me is purely professional – for lots of reasons.'

'Which are, Monsieur Clare?'

John Clare stood up and faced the policeman. 'One: I don't like to get involved with people I work with. Two: I'm not attracted to Hakim in that way. And three . . . he's not gay.'

'Sounds reasonable to me, Captain,' I said.

After the interview I couldn't wait to give Captain Lefèvre my two-pennorth. Before we'd reached the top of the stairs I'd criticised him for the way he'd handled John Clare, questioned his reasons for detaining him and called him *un ignorant* – an ignoramus.

He stopped when we reached the foyer.

A post-mortem, he told me, had revealed Rougeard's time of death to be no later than the previous Wednesday, the day after Hakim Wattar had been released. He added that Wattar had also resisted arrest that morning and that certain evidence, possibly stolen from Rougeard's property, had been found in the Algerian's flat. As for John Clare, it was quite normal, he said, to interrogate the known associates of a suspected murderer.

Apparently I was the ignoramus.

I accepted Lefèvre's offer to walk me back to the car. We

were still friends, it seemed.

A police Peugeot parked directly in front of the entrance made me think the injured man whom I'd seen that morning, shoehorned in the back of the same vehicle.

'Hakim Wattar,' I said. 'Did you arrest him this morning, at about nine a.m.?'

'How do you know that?'

'Oh, I was driving past on my way back from the college. He looked as though he'd been beaten up.'

I looked at Lefèvre. What had he said – *resisted arrest*?

He laughed, then stopped himself abruptly, fixing a serious expression. 'No, Jeanne. Not at all. It is like this, okay: we were talking to the owner of the bar this morning about Wattar when the man himself came in. I asked him, "Do you know René Rougeard?" and he said, "What, that *sale con!*" I told him not to speak ill of the dead and he looked at me as if he had just seen a ghost, then ran from the bar.'

'So how did he get injured then?'

'It was raining ropes. We pursued Hakim across the street. He slipped and fell onto the kerbstone, bruised his head and broke one of his teeth.'

His response sounded far too well rehearsed. Pierre Lefèvre, I said to myself, the more I learn, the less I like.

He must have read my mind.

'No, honestly,' he said. 'No one in the station could believe it when I brought Wattar in – I do not have much of a reputation for being, you know . . . physical. I must have repeated the story a dozen times this morning, including to the *Inspection Générale* – the Internal Affairs boys.'

Okay, Lefèvre, I'll believe you, thousands wouldn't. 'And what does Hakim say?'

'Not much, at present. He refuses to talk until we get an interpreter. Our usual Arabic translator is still on vacation.'

What I said next I regretted immediately.

39

'I could ask my new apprentice to help, if you like.'

Loubna is a shy, quiet girl. So, while waiting for her in the University car park, I'd been feeling apprehensive about involving her in Lefèvre's investigation. But when I asked if she'd mind acting as an interpreter for Wattar she became unusually animated. Archie seemed excited too. The two of them, I learned, were gangster movie fans.

I dropped Archie off at home, with instructions to feed the dog and tell Wendy what was going on, then returned to the *hôtel de police*.

Again, Lefèvre was waiting for us on the steps. I introduced him to Loubna, and the three of us went downstairs.

Another green door to a windowless room, another Formica table – this time occupied by a bald, exhausted-looking North African. Standing behind him was a uniformed guard.

'*Merci, Jonzac,*' said Lefèvre.

'*Capitaine.*'

Lefèvre waited for the guard to close the door on his way out before speaking again.

'Monsieur Wattar, this lady is Madame Valeix. She is a friend of John Clare, and this is . . .'

'Loubna Ben Moumen,' the girl said.

The sound of Loubna's voice changed Wattar's demeanour entirely. He stood up and shook her hand enthusiastically, smiling. '*Salam alaikum,*' he said, softly.

'*Alaikum salam*,' she replied.

Wattar began to speak. He talked at length, steadily but with a hurried pace. Loubna listened attentively and waited for the man to finish. When he had, he sat back down, his eyes fixed on Loubna's face.

I'd never seen a man look more frightened. Loubna seemed confused.

'Well, Mademoiselle?'

She began, slowly, to relate Wattar's words.

'Monsieur Wattar is very frightened. He believes he has been cursed by one of the jinn – a demon, I think you say. The demon came to him on the feast day of Eid-al-Fitr, gave him wine and tempted him to drink it. In the night, when Monsieur had taken the wine, the demon returned. He held a knife to Monsieur's throat and threatened to execute him for his sinful drinking, saying—'

She turned to Wattar and questioned him. Wattar's reply was, for Lefèvre and me, unintelligible, but the sound the words made was captivating – tuneful, rhythmic and forlorn. She translated: '"Whoever disobeys God and His Messenger then for him is the fire of Hell; they will abide therein forever." Monsieur says he begged for forgiveness and the demon said he would spare him if—'

Again, she clarified something with the man. When he had finished she said, 'I am not so familiar with this verse.'

I guessed that Wattar was reciting some sort of religious text.

'He's saying something like "wait for them to come in the shadows of the clouds" and "the case would be already judged".'

It was Lefèvre's turn to speak. 'Monsieur Wattar,' he said, 'did you visit Château Lacasse after you were released from the *gendarmerie*?'

Wattar clearly understood the question and shook his head. '*Non, monsieur,*' he said.

'Did you steal wine from Monsieur Rougeard – the bottles we found in your flat?'

Again a headshake. '*Non, monsieur.*'

'Did you murder Monsieur Rougeard, young man?'

'*Non.*'

'Monsieur Wattar, you must answer all my questions truthfully, otherwise you will be detained here at the *hôtel de police* for a long time. Do you understand?'

'*Oui, monsieur! Merci, monsieur!*'

Wattar proceeded to address the policeman in his mother tongue then fell silent. Again, Loubna translated:

'He would like to thank you, Captain, for your hospitality. He will be happy here in Libourne.'

A smile slid across Lefèvre's face. 'That is the first time anyone ever said that!'

Again Wattar spoke, this time his words sounded harsh, as though he were spitting them out.

Lefèvre and I both looked at Loubna.

'He says the jinn are out there, Captain. He feels safer here.'

The interview continued for nearly an hour. Lefèvre wanted to know the exact details of Wattar's movements following his arrest in Les Eglisottes. He also asked Wattar to clarify the seemingly supernatural experiences he'd endured on the day of Eid-al-Fitr, the holy feast that marks the end of Ramadan. Could Wattar's encounter with the jinn be merely a hunger-induced hallucination caused by a month of fasting, heightened by alcohol? Wattar didn't think so, and nor could he provide any other account of how the bottles of wine, all missing from Rougeard's inventory, had come to be in his possession. However, his description of the demon's appearance was vividly compelling: a large, hooded man with burning red eyes. He described the smell of death that clung to the demon's white clothing and his deep voice, sinister and threatening. The phrases Wattar used – lines from the Quran – could have been recited from memory, but he swore on the holy book itself that the demon had spoken the words to him. Why had he run when Lefèvre had questioned him? Six days after his visitation, the demon's prophecy had, it seemed to Wattar, come true: *wait for them to come in the shadows of the clouds ... the case would already be judged.* His ex-boss was dead. A policeman had come to give him the news after a torrential rainstorm. He had already been judged.

We said our goodbyes.

'*Ma'a salama, Mademoiselle,*' Wattar whispered to Loubna, then added something else – a lost line of mournful, poetic Arabic.

We left Lefèvre at the door of the station and strolled back towards the car. I was curious to know what Loubna thought about Hakim Wattar's drinking.

'The Holy Quran says that to be intoxicated is a sin against God. Alcohol is an intoxicant, so therefore it is forbidden, and therefore Hakim Wattar is a sinner.'

A sinner, maybe, but Wattar's familiarity with the word of God was, for me, perplexing. 'But he seems so . . . devout.'

'Only God is perfect, Jeanne. No man is.'

I was struck by the logical simplicity of Loubna's answer. How then, I wondered, had the Ben Moumen family reconciled their faith with winemaking? If only people were as logical and perfect as the religions they create.

When we got back to the car I asked Loubna what Wattar had whispered to her. Her gorgeous green eyes scanned the streetscape then focussed on me.

'And unto God are all affairs returned,' she said.

I shivered, thinking about Hakim Wattar's white-robed intruder.

'How about pizza for dinner, Loubna?'

'Cool.'

Mardi 6 Séptembre 2011

On Tuesday morning, the last of summer's swallows were hurtling over the vine tops under a picture-postcard blue sky. Yesterday's storms had cleared the air, but my thoughts were far from clear. I couldn't believe that the quietly spoken Algerian had killed Rougeard. I could, perhaps, imagine a more powerful man dragging his victim to a grisly death atop that winery scaffold, but not Hakim Wattar. And as for John Clare's involvement, I was even more sceptical. Besides his quiet manners and convincing testimony, Clare was a winemaker, a man who spent endless hours tending his precious vines. Would he have deliberately wasted over six thousand litres of wine? I didn't think so; we winemakers care about wine. We rely on a single annual crop for our livelihood. We respect it, worry about it. On the evening following Clare's discovery of a savagely murdered corpse, he was worrying about the forthcoming harvest. I've misjudged people in the past, but I was convinced of one thing – John Clare had not killed René Rougeard.

I stood in the open doorway of the tractor hangar, a bit out of breath after cleaning and tidying a year's accumulated clutter, inhaling the warm, vine-scented air of the vineyard. Behind me all was spick and span. In front of me was a valley full of nearly ripe grapes. In less than two weeks my vats would be full of this year's vintage and I could relax, loosen anxiety's grip – at least until next year.

I'm always like this at harvest time. I worry. I fret. Right now, Lefèvre's murder investigation was the last thing I needed.

I'd arranged to pick up Archie and Loubna after college, so at just before six I rolled back Clémentine's cloth roof and drove into Libourne.

Archie, for all his extraordinary mental abilities, is a terribly nervous driver. He passed his driving test in England but refuses to drive on French roads. Loubna, according to her CV, had a full Moroccan driving licence. But so far she'd been reluctant to drive either the Citroën or my 4x4. She too was nervous, she said, about driving in France. Doubtless the roads around Bordeaux seemed daunting to a girl more used to the quiet country lanes and mountain tracks of her homeland. I put it down to her shyness; she just needed time to settle in. Still, I hoped she'd be ready to drive the vineyard tractor in a week's time.

'It's specified in parts per million, Jeanne,' Archie was telling me, from the 2CV's back seat.

'We have been learning about the sulphur dioxide in wine,' Loubna explained.

I jammed the quirky gear shift into first and pulled out of the University car park. 'Sounds interesting, Loubna.'

'Yes,' Archie said, 'even organic wines contain what they call *bound* sulphur in concentrations of up to ten parts per million, but levels of up to one hundred and sixty are—'

'Archie,' I interrupted, 'you're not going to give us the chemical formulas are you?'

'Formul*ae*, Jeanne.'

'Okay, formul*ae*.'

'No, I'm not,' he said. I looked in the rear view mirror. Turk was licking the boy's ear.

Loubna continued. 'Archie was incredible, Jeanne. Our *professeur* gave us seven wines to taste, each containing different levels of sulphur dioxide. Archie could tell *exactly* how much there was in each wine.'

'Okay, Archie,' I said, addressing the mirror. 'How did you do that?'

'Well, you know,' he said, 'the smell of sulphur has a colour. I see it like a layer of mist – like the way the morning mist hangs over the vines? – and the stronger it is, the deeper it is.'

'I see,' I lied.

'So, once I know what a one-part-per-million smell is, I can guess the concentration of other smells.'

Archie's synaesthesia has always been a joyous mystery to me.

I stopped at a junction and glanced at him again; God, he looked like his dad. Apart from his smooth chin and pale blue eyes, he was the image of Andrew. You're a one in a million, Archie, I thought.

'So, what colour is the smell of sulphur then?'

'White,' he said.

We were back in a stream of homebound traffic on the Cours Tourny. Driving past the *hôtel de police* I wondered if John Clare might still be there, answering questions in the subterranean interview room. I hadn't told him that my grape pickers were available to harvest his vineyards, and I made a mental note to contact him when we got home.

The phone was answered on the first ring.

'*Allo?*'

'John? It's Jeanne Valeix.'

'Oh, hi, Jeanne. I'm sorry. I was expecting someone else.' I could hear a loud, low-pitched growling followed by couple of excited yelps. 'Excuse the noise – it's feeding time at the zoo.'

'Sorry, have I called at a bad time?'

'No, no. It's good to hear from you. Just a minute—' The animal noises abated and I heard the sound of a door slam. '—that's better. How are you?'

'I'm fine, John, but how are *you*?'

'I'm okay now the French authorities no longer think I'm a murderer.'

'They let you go then? I mean, without charging you?'

'No choice. They think Rougeard was killed on Wednesday evening when I was at a dinner party with a friend of mine, Philippe – he's an *avocat*, from Paris. Apparently the police accept my alibi.'

'Oh, that's great, John. But what about Hakim Wattar?'

'Ah, that's why I'm waiting for a phone call – from my friend, you see. He thinks he can get Hakim released. Someone is clearly trying to frame him.'

'Have you seen him – Hakim, I mean?'

'Yeah, they let me see him before chucking me out last night. He's very scared.'

'He seemed reluctant to leave police custody when I saw him yesterday.'

'Yeah, but I'm sure he'll feel safe here with Priscilla and Dorothy.'

'Who? Oh, yes, you have dogs. What are they?'

'Dobermans. I don't worry about intruders.'

For a moment we, and the dogs, were silent. Then I remembered why I was calling.

'Ah, yes. My grape pickers can be with you on the 16th if you need them.'

'Oh, that's wonderful news, Jeanne. No one's seen hide nor hair of my usual lot . . .'

Again, silence.

'Who do you think did it, John?' I asked.

'God knows . . . They say Rougeard was a gambler, in spite of his churchy ways. Maybe The Mafia were after him. I don't know.'

I couldn't imagine a gang of Sicilian mobsters killing a country winemaker in the middle of rural France, but – who knows? – stranger things have happened. 'What do the police think now?'

'I think they're looking at the gambling angle, but at

the moment the only evidence they have points to Hakim.'

'Oh, well,' I said, 'let's hope your friend the advocate can get him released.'

'I'm sure he will. And let's hope your friend the captain can catch who's really responsible, eh?'

We said goodbye.

Yes, I thought, for Hakim Wattar's sake, let's hope so.

As soon as I put the phone down it rang. It was Captain Lefèvre.

'*Bonsoir,* Jeanne,' he said.

We exchanged pleasantries, and he asked if I was free for dinner.

I thought about it; he still owed me one. 'That depends. What did you have in mind, Pierre?'

'How about the casino?'

'I didn't know you were a gambler, *Capitaine.*'

'There are many things you do not know about me, Jeanne. But there's more to the Casino than roulette and blackjack.'

'I'm intrigued, Pierre. Like what?'

'A good restaurant, for one thing.'

'Mmm, that sounds nice.'

'You'll come then?' – I didn't say anything – 'I could pick you up at eight-thirty?'

'Okay, Pierre,' I said.

'*Génial!* See you later.'

'*A tout à l'heure.*'

I'd forgotten that Archie had offered to cook supper.

'Don't worry about me, my gorgeous girl. I'll just sit here and read an unimproving book.'

Wendy, who had developed a penchant for erotic novellas, was relaxing on the sofa wearing a blue silk kimono and a pair of furry slippers. She assured me Archie wouldn't be offended if I went out; and anyway, he and Loubna had plans: they intended to watch a film together after dinner.

I weighed up the alternatives: stodgy pasta followed by the sound of gunfire and expletives blaring from the TV set, or a civilised dinner with Pierre Lefèvre at the casino.

I plumped for the casino.

Once again I was crossing the Gironde in Pierre's Peugeot 407, this time heading west. A fishing boat, carried by the outgoing tide, chugged its way towards the sea. I thought about how little I knew of Lefèvre's private life. He was a single man in his forties, he liked French opera and he lived alone; that was all. He could be anything for goodness' sake – a cross-dresser, a naturist, some sort of religious fundamentalist. For all I knew he was gay.

He squinted into the lowering sun, flipped the visor down, his hand moving back to the steering wheel in a slow, delicate movement. Soft hairs shone gold against the bronze of his suntanned forearms. I looked at his face: crinkly eyes; short, tidy brown hair, greying at the sides; a square, tense jaw; a day's beard growth. Somehow I couldn't see him wearing makeup; no amount of foundation could conceal *that* stubble. Nor could I imagine him strolling naked along a wind-swept beach (well, okay, I could). Nor did I think he was a Scientologist.

Was he gay? Well, maybe – he wasn't married after all.

I couldn't contain my curiosity.

'Were you ever married, Pierre?'

He threw me a glance. 'Me? Married? No, I have never been married, Jeanne. Married to my job, maybe.'

He glanced over his left shoulder and overtook a tanker truck. 'Funny, that expression: "married to the job". It is what they say in American cop films, *n'est-ce pas?* Why is it always cops? Why not plumbers . . . librarians . . . what's the word – *poissonniers?*'

'Fishmongers.'

'Yes, fishmongers. Are they not just as dedicated to their jobs?'

49

'I suppose filmmakers think police work is more exciting. I can't imagine a thriller about a fishmonger.'

He flashed me a bright smile. 'The Cod Father?'

I laughed. 'Not bad, Pierre. You're English is getting better all the time.'

'I have a good teacher,' he said.

Another big smile.

'Beverly Hills Carp,' I said.

'*Ah, c'est trop fort!*' he said, his shoulders heaving. 'Very funny. And it works in French, too, you know.'

Sighs replaced our laughter, and we sat there, side-by-side, staring at the dual carriageway ahead.

'So, was there never anyone . . . you know, special?'

He sighed again.

'Yes, there was someone, once. A long, long time ago.'

I kept quiet, waiting, watching his fingers caress the wheel when he steered past another truck.

'She was – *is* – an artist, a painter. I thought she was the one, you know. She made so many portraits of me. Painting me into her heart, she said – can you believe it? The things we say when we are young . . . Anyway, I could not see it then, but she grew tired of me – as a lover and as a subject, I suppose. She left me and hooked up with a colleague of mine – my best friend, at the time.'

'Oh, that's awful, Pierre, how did you cope – at work, I mean?'

'He was transferred to Bordeaux shortly afterwards and they moved to the city. One night, I bumped into him outside a Vietnamese restaurant and we fought – like schoolboys, rolling around in the street. I hated him so much. That night I lay awake, wishing he was dead. I forget what happened the week after the fight, but the following weekend my wish was granted. He was shot in the chest by a small-time crook during a drugs raid.'

Oh, my, God. I shifted in my seat, turned to face him. 'I don't know what to say, Pierre. You must have been devastated.'

He sighed. 'I decided that my feelings did not count for much. I had lost my *copine* and my best friend, but at least I was alive. She moved away, to Toulouse, I think. Since then—' He flicked the indicator and looked at me for a split second. 'I have never met the right person. Although . . .'

We came off the autoroute, following the slip road towards a nondescript commercial zone, not far from the river.

'Although what?' I asked.

'I am still . . . hopeful.'

His smile returned. The car orbited a mini roundabout with the left indicator clicking.

'Marcel Bonami, that was his name. *Bon ami*: good friend. Not much of a good friend, eh? Of course, I forgave him – and her, eventually. I never forgave myself, though. Ah, here we are.'

Lefèvre swung into a parking bay next to a silver sports. I'm no expert on cars, but this one looked expensive.

We got out. The door locks clicked with a loud beep and a flash of the lights.

'Looks like the boss is here,' Lefèvre said, eyeing the adjacent car. Something about its registration plate was familiar. Above the numbers and letters was the name of the dealership – Victor Lemaitre Mercedes – followed by a stylized picture of a fork-bearing devil. I'd seen one of Lemaitre's cars somewhere before, recently. Then I remembered: Rougeard's vehicle's plates bore the same logo.

I'm not sure what I was expecting (the out-of-town setting should have given me a clue), but the casino was a bit of a letdown. I'd imagined a grand nineteenth-century palace with wealthy clients arriving by limousine, brocaded commissionaires and art nouveau décor. You know, high heels and low tops; the smell of cheap cigars and expensive perfume; bourgeois France at its most louche.

Disappointingly, the place looked more like an airport conference centre and smelled of carpet cleaner.

Still, at least they had palm trees.

I don't recall exactly what we ate that evening, or the details of our conversation. Lefèvre seemed somewhat distant – the way he had been on Sunday night on the way home. Tense and pensive.

By the time our desserts arrived Lefèvre had clearly lost his appetite. He was chasing a couple of raspberries around the plate when his attention was drawn to a group of men making their way over to a cocktail bar at the far end of the dining room.

'*Excusez-moi*, Jeanne,' he said, 'just for a few moments.'

'I—' I began, watching him walk past me in the direction of the bar. I twisted round, curious to know what was going on. The barman had served the group what looked like shots of whisky, and the men were chatting affably. One of them, older than the others and distinguishable by his ruddy complexion and barrel-chested frame, spotted the captain and hesitated mid-sentence. Clearly, they knew each other because he grasped Lefèvre's right hand with both of his in a magnanimous handshake. I couldn't hear the conversation, but introductions were made, then the red-faced man put his arm round Lefèvre's shoulders and steered him towards our table.

So, I thought, perhaps now we'll find out the real reason for dinner at the casino.

'. . . but first,' the man was saying, 'you must introduce me to your guest, *Capitaine*.'

'*Monsieur*, this is my friend, Jeanne Valeix. Jeanne, this is Monsieur Lemaitre, the owner of the casino.'

'*Enchanté, madame, et bon appétit.* Please, call me Victor.'

Ah, and a car dealer, too, I thought. He took my hand,

raising it to his moustachioed lips to kiss, squinting at me through bushy eyebrows. I can't remember ever having been kissed on the hand before; in a funny way, I almost enjoyed it.

Somewhere, sometime, I'd seen Victor Lemaitre before.

'Haven't we met?' I asked.

'I am absolutely sure we have not, *madame*. I rarely forget a face and never one as beautiful as yours.'

I wrested my hand from his sweaty grip. Louche, I said to myself, would describe you to a tee.

Lefèvre looked edgy.

Lemaitre turned his attention from me back to the captain. 'So, what was it you wanted to discuss?'

'Er, you may have heard about the murder near Libourne.'

'Well, yes, of course, the papers have been full of little else this week, but—' He lowered his voice and leaned closer to Lefèvre. '—Xavier informed me that the victim was . . . a regular visitor here. Although he did not reveal any of the details, of course.'

'Of course,' Lefèvre said. 'Well, we are following a number of lines of enquiry, and since I am here—'

'Yes, since you are here,' Lemaitre interrupted, 'you would naturally like to know what sort of a client your murder victim was?'

Lefèvre nodded.

'Well, that's no problem, I'm sure. We can go and have a look at the man's account if you like?'

Lefèvre looked relieved. 'Thank you, *monsieur*. Jeanne, if you don't mind, Monsieur Lemaitre and I will—'

Again, Lemaitre interrupted. 'You're not going to abandon your guest, are you? Madame Valeix can accompany us, Lefèvre.'

'Yes, but—'

'*Bien*. So, shall we go to my office and look-up Monsieur . . . Roget, was it?'

'Rougeard,' Lefèvre corrected.

We followed Lemaitre through the dining room towards a door marked *PRIVÉ*. The men at the bar looked at us as we passed. One in particular, a burly, dark-suited man, raised his eyebrows questioningly at Lemaitre who gestured to him, palms down. 'You stay here and enjoy your drinks, *messieurs*,' he said.

We exited through the door and climbed a double flight of stairs to Victor Lemaitre's office.

His desk was cluttered with silver-framed photographs of the man himself standing beside, or playing golf with, French politicians and minor celebrities. Lefèvre asked politely how the pre-election campaigning was going, and we learned that Victor Lemaitre was tipped to become Libourne's next mayor.

As well as the framed photos, the desk was home to a large computer screen displaying a slideshow of pictures – mostly of Lemaitre in various sports cars. Fixed to the wall behind were several more screens, but these showed CCTV images of the blackjack, boule and roulette tables, and views of the car park, bar area and dining room. I noticed that one of the screens showed our vacant table: two abandoned desserts waiting for their diners to return.

Lemaitre picked up a phone and ordered coffee, gesturing to us mutely to be seated. A female croupier arrived with our drinks. His gaze followed the girl – an Asian beauty – as she turned and left the room, closing the door softly behind her.

We sipped our coffees while Lemaitre tapped a few buttons on the computer's keyboard.

'*Alors* . . . Rougeard – R, O, U, G . . . Ah, here we are: Rougeard, René, Château Lacasse, Les Eglisottes.'

He swivelled the computer screen round so Lefèvre could read it more easily.

'As you can see, *Capitaine*, Monsieur Rougeard was a good client. He always paid his gambling debts and he was enjoying quite a lucky streak recently.' He poked the screen with his little finger. 'See, here, his account is still in credit.

'I can print out these figures for you, of course. Now, if there's nothing else, may I return to my guests?'

Lefevre's attention shifted from the screen to its owner. 'His luck ran out last week, though.'

'I'm sorry?'

'You said he was enjoying a lucky streak.'

'Ah, yes. Indeed.'

'Did you know René Rougeard, *monsieur*?'

'Know him? Personally? No, I don't believe we ever met.'

'Do you have any reason to believe that Rougeard was in trouble – financially, I mean?'

'Look, Lefèvre, you can see his financial dealings with us here in black and white, and I've already told you that I didn't know him. I don't associate with all our clients, you understand.'

'No, indeed.' Lefèvre said, writing something down in a small notepad. 'Can you tell me, though, the date of his last visit here?'

Lemaitre clicked a few more keys. 'Friday the 26th, last month.'

Again, Lefèvre scribbled.

'Thank you, Monsieur Lemaitre,' he said, standing. 'By the way, do you keep video tapes of all these security monitors?'

'We keep them for a week, after which they are re-recorded.'

'So, you wouldn't have the tapes from the night of the 26th?'

'No, I'm sorry. I'm afraid not.'

We walked slowly back to the car park in the warm glow cast by the floodlit palm trees. Myriad tree frogs serenaded each other somewhere in the shimmering fronds above our heads.

Up ahead I saw the silhouette of a hooded, well-built

figure walking towards us – a bouncer, perhaps, starting his nightshift. Instinctively I linked arms with Lefèvre.

'Who's Xavier?' I asked.

Lefèvre grunted. 'My commandant, Xavier Foliot. Monsieur Lemaitre's son-in-law.'

'A friend of yours?' I asked.

'No, he is not a friend.'

'A rival then?'

His response hardly answered my question. 'I shot a man once,' he said. 'Well, twice in fact.'

He stopped and put out his hand to touch the hairy scales on a palm tree's trunk.

'You've shot two men?'

'No, I shot the same man twice, once in each leg.'

'I see,' I said, untruthfully. 'That seems a little . . . excessive.'

'He was running towards me wielding a samurai sword.'

I looked at his dark face; he was deadly serious.

'So I shot him,' he said, 'in the right leg.'

We turned and continued our stroll back towards the car park.

'That didn't stop him,' he went on, 'so I shot him in the other leg. *That* stopped him.'

I wanted to laugh, but Lefèvre's expression remained fixed in a rueful scowl.

'I have Xavier Foliot to thank for the incident and the legal and professional proceedings which followed.'

'How is that?' I asked.

Again he stopped.

'Foliot knew that the man kept a small armoury of illegal weapons. He also knew he was mentally unstable. He failed to report any of this to my unit when we were called to arrest the man, because Foliot was taking bribes from him.

'But, he is still a colleague, still working for the Police?'

'I could prove nothing, and Foliot got away with only

a slap on the wrist. Like I say, his father-in-law is the future mayor. Friends in high places.'

We reached the end of the avenue. I was puzzled that the lone man I'd seen approaching us had completely vanished. While Lefèvre searched his pockets for the car keys, I looked over my shoulder at the deserted walkway between us and the casino. The frogs had stopped chirruping. I'm not normally susceptible to such things but, just for a moment, I had the overwhelming feeling that the hooded figure was watching us, somewhere among the shadows behind the trees.

Except for Turk, curled up in his basket, no one was about when I got home.

I tiptoed quietly to the bathroom past Wendy's door (the sound of snoring) and Archie's (suppressed giggles). So, I thought, looks like Archie and Loubna have made friends.

Our antediluvian boiler was playing up again, and the water in the pipes was stone cold. So, dressed in my bathrobe and slippers, I went down to the boiler house to investigate.

The rusty latch on the boiler house door snagged my finger, and I sucked the grazed skin, cursing myself for forgetting the torch. Inside was as black as the hobs of hell. I flicked the light switch – nothing. Now I had a blown fuse to fix as well as a dodgy boiler. Where was the man of the house when you needed one?

A faint rustling noise, somewhere in the darkness, quickened my pulse. 'Mice,' I whispered, shuffling blindly forward, arms outstretched, zombie-like, until my fingers touched the boiler's cold metal casing. I reached up to an eye-level shelf where the matches are kept.

Again, the faint rustling, scratching noise.

When the match spluttered into life, flooding the room with phosphorus light, a white creature, all feathers and claws, flew past me, inches from my horror-stricken face. We both screeched and the creature escaped into the night through a gap between the eaves and the old stone wall.

I don't know which of us was more scared: me or the owl.

After my breathing and my heart rate had steadied, I examined the boiler. The pilot light had gone out, and it took me a good ten minutes and countless matches to relight it.

A nightmare.

A white-clad, hooded figure with burning red eyes appeared at my bedside. His hands, reaching out to me through the semi-darkness, were like two scaly claws; his tunic was festooned with a million white feathers. He spoke a guttural foreign language I couldn't understand. When the claws closed around my mouth and neck, I could smell the creature's fetid breath – the white smell of sulphur, the smell of death.

Mercredi 7 Séptembre 2011

I opened my eyes, squinting into the brightness. Beside me on the pillow was a white barn owl feather.

The young people had left for college when I came down for breakfast. I was amazed when Wendy told me that Archie had offered to drive. Taking his 'new girlfriend' to school was how she'd put it. It looked as though Loubna's charms had boosted the boy's confidence, and I was pleased for them both.

Wendy asked me about my evening with the captain. Less memorable, was the best I could say about it. No corpses this time, but no kiss either: we'd arrived home, discussed René Rougeard's gambling, and agreed to meet up at the *hôtel de police* in the morning. Lefèvre wanted to ask me about the dead man's business accounts.

This time we met in the reception area then went upstairs to an open-plan squad room. The room contained ten-or-so desks, most of which were in use.

The men – they were all men – stared at us. Lefèvre muttered a vague acknowledgement to his colleagues before ushering me into a glass-walled office.

A man appeared on the other side of the door. He looked at us, smiling, then knocked with the back of his hand. His wedding ring made a loud tapping noise on the glass.

'*Mon dieu,*' Lefèvre whispered under his breath, then opened the door and allowed the man to enter.

'*Bonjour, madame,*' he said, still smiling. He was a clean-cut type and handsome, too, I suppose; but something about the over-confident way he looked at me when he took my hand put me on my guard. I hate to pigeonhole a man by his appearance, but this one just looked plain shifty.

'*Enchantée,*' I lied. 'I'm—'

'Lefèvre, you never said your girlfriend was so beautiful. Your luck must be better than your looks, no?'

Lefèvre forced a thin smile.

'We all thought Lefèvre was . . . well, you know, that he didn't like the ladies!' He laughed, clapping Lefèvre on the back. 'Oh, it's just a joke, Madame. Barrack room humour, *n'est-ce pas,* Pierre?'

'Well, sir, now that you have met my *friend*, perhaps you will—'

'Met?' the man said. 'You haven't even introduced us!'

Lefèvre sighed. 'Madame Valeix, this is Commandant Xavier Foliot.'

'*Enchanté*, Madame Valeix,' Foliot said, giving me a low bow – an affectation that did nothing to improve my poor first impressions. I noticed a bald patch the size of a two euro coin on the top of his head over which he'd combed his dark, greasy hair.

So, I thought, this is Pierre's rival.

A younger man appeared at the open door of the little office and beckoned to Foliot. 'Boss wants to see you, Commandant.'

Foliot excused himself and went out. I waited until the door clicked shut.

'What a creep,' I said. 'What did he mean by *girlfriend*?'

Lefèvre's cheeks coloured, ever so slightly. 'Oh, you know, the boys were asking about you and . . . I never said *girlfriend*. I didn't use that word. I don't know where Foliot got *that* from . . .'

I was confused but flattered and a little excited that

Lefèvre might think that our relationship was more than just professional. I was also annoyed that he'd been discussing me with his colleagues. Confused, flattered, excited and annoyed: a volatile emotional cocktail.

'Pierre, why am I here? I mean, why have you involved me in all this?'

'You are my expert witness, Jeanne. Rougeard's computer and paper files were missing. I thought you might be able to help me understand his business dealings. Plus, with Lieutenant Dauzac away, you are helping me greatly with the investigation.'

He was embarrassed, and his smile was doing a terrible job to conceal it.

I, on the other hand, have never felt awkward in situations like these – never backward about coming forward, as my mother always used to say.

'Why don't you tell me the real reason, Pierre?'

He continued to look uncomfortable. 'The real reason for what?'

'The real reason why your archrival Xavier what's-his-name thinks I'm your girlfriend.'

I glanced through the glass partition at the office beyond. All but one or two of the men were looking in our direction. Lefèvre went silently over to the door, closed a louvered blind, then removed some papers from a cardboard file on the desk.

I'd have preferred a more romantic setting than the soulless meeting room, but at least he'd closed the blinds. But, I thought, if Pierre is finally going to declare his feelings for me, then he might as well do it here as anywhere else. I smiled, then shot him a glance straight between the eyes.

'You want them to think I'm your girlfriend, don't you, Pierre?'

Again silence. Perhaps he was just too timid.

'Well, don't you?'

His brow ruckled into a scowl. He blushed.

'Yes,' he said, sighing, collapsing into a swivel chair.

I sat down opposite and waited for him to continue.

'Well?' I prompted.

'Well, as you know, I am a single man.'

I wondered if he could hear my heart pounding because I could. 'Yes . . .'

'A single man, of my age, is an outsider in the police, a figure of fun, you know. People say things.'

I didn't understand. 'What things?' I asked.

'Well, with Dauzac being—' He was still shuffling the paperwork, avoiding my gaze. '—the way he is.'

I'd met Lieutenant Dauzac several times. He'd always struck me as a nice young man and a fine policeman. 'You mean because he's black?'

Lefèvre looked up at me, seemingly more confused than I was. 'No, no, not that; because he is – *gay.*'

Now I was really confused.

'I don't see—' I began, and then it hit me. My smile faded. My jaw dropped. Jeanne, I said to myself, what a damn fool you are. 'Hold on, you want your colleagues to think I'm your girlfriend so they don't think you're gay?'

'Well, I would not put it like that, Jeanne, no. And please believe me, I . . . I need your help.' He was almost pleading with me and I was almost buying it – almost.

'Well, don't count on it from now on, Captain,' I said, and turned to leave.

'But, Jeanne, I just thought, as we are friends—'

'Don't, Pierre. Just don't think *anything.*'

He exhaled another long sigh. 'Now it is you,' he muttered.

Only curiosity prevented me from opening the door and storming out. 'What?' I said.

He stared up at the tube lights in the ceiling. 'I am in trouble with Internal Affairs because of Wattar, and with my boss for bothering Lemaitre last night . . .' His expression, when he looked back at me, was tragic. 'The chief wants a charge before the Jurade—apparently this year there will be a lot of media coverage. He has given me until next Monday to come up with a water-tight arrest;

otherwise he will pass the case to Foliot. I only have one very unlikely suspect who will have to be released later today. And now? Now I am in trouble with you, Jeanne.'

He fished out the remainder of the papers from the file, then reached inside and lifted out a clear plastic evidence bag containing a red-topped wine bottle. I recognised the label – the plain design; the gold lettering on a white background; a pair of gold medals bracketing the prestigious name: Château Cheval Blanc. The wine in the bag was Saint-Emilion's finest and most expensive claret.

'All I have,' he concluded, weighing the bottle in his hand, 'is a few clues, no real suspects and one bottle of evidence.'

Now I was even more curious. I'd assumed that the stolen wine found at Hakim Wattar's place was Rougeard's own produce, but this was something else: rare, famous, hugely expensive, and from an excellent vintage. Only a couple of days ago, at lunch at Chèz Stéphane, this wine had cropped up in conversation. What had Stéphane said about black-market wine? A certain *grand cru classé* was changing hands on Bordeaux's black market for only fifty euros a bottle – Château Cheval Blanc '90, apparently. Could the wine in Lefèvre's evidence bag come from the same batch Stéphane had mentioned?

I wasn't in the mood to give Lefèvre any more of my time, and I certainly wasn't going to tell him what Stéphane had said; he would have to find that out for himself.

His face bore a hangdog look when I turned to say goodbye.

'I'm in the dog kennel with everyone,' he said.

He meant *doghouse*. Men, I thought: if you didn't pity them you'd have to hate them.

'Goodbye, Pierre,' I said, trying not to flounce as I walked out. The men in the squad room fell silent, all taking pains not to stare at me.

I took the back route from Libourne to Saint-Emilion, impatiently flicking the radio dial from one awful Euro-pop station to another. Motoring past the southern corner of Cheval Blanc's vineyards, one song caught my attention; the music, though mournful, was more to my taste, and the singer's voice reminded me of Lefèvre's.

> *Elle m'en veut*
> *De mettre de l'eau*
> *Dans son vin, dans ses yeux*

She's fed *up with me*, the song went, *for putting water in her wine, and in her eyes.*

I pulled over to the side of the road, my eyes bleary with tears put there by Pierre Lefèvre.

Jeudi 8 Séptembre 2011

'I'm going into Bordeaux after breakfast, Wendy. Can I get you anything?'

'What's that, my gorgeous?'

She was at the open door, bringing in a handful of letters. I waited for the noisy post van to drive off. 'Do you need anything from Bordeaux?'

'Need?' Wendy replied. 'What could I possibly need? At my time of life you don't acquire things, you get rid of them. You know – houses, books, brain cells . . .'

I swallowed the rest of my toasted brioche and downed the last of the coffee.

'What about your *Guardian*?'

'Oh, thank you, my dear. Yes, that would be lovely – you won't have to go out of your way?'

'No, not at all.'

I opened the mail, then began to tidy away the breakfast things.

'Why are you going into town, anyway?' she asked.

'To see the accountant,' I lied.

I'd telephoned Stéphane Lavergne the previous evening to ask him who was selling the illicit Cheval Blanc. Stéphane couldn't tell me the man's real name, only that he was known to his associates as Le Blaireau – The Badger. He lived in a scruffy suburb on the south side of the city and spent most of his time in the bookmakers-stroke-bar called the PMU. Le Blaireau sounded scary to me, but apparently he was harmless: a sixty-something small-time wine dealer. He shared his moniker with a famous French cyclist because, so the story went, he'd once competed in the Tour de France. Ironically, the man was confined to a wheelchair.

That morning I'd decided to pay Le Blaireau a visit. My hunch was that some of Rougeard's stolen wine had made it onto Bordeaux's black market. But with Lefèvre still in my bad books, I couldn't tell him my theory. What the hell, I thought. After all, what harm can a badger in a wheelchair do?

One day I'll stop underestimating risk, stop acting on impulse. One day.

I applied the brakes, squinting over the hinge in Clémentine's side window. Finding the PMU was proving tricky. I wasn't familiar with this end of town, and the low-rise streets all looked the same. I'd passed several bars, any of which could have been Le Blaireau's HQ, but none bore the emblem of France's state-owned bookmakers.

Headlights flashed in my mirror, and the impatient driver behind me hit the horn. I gave up, pulled in at the kerbside and cut the engine.

I hadn't noticed it on my drive past, but there, a couple of hundred metres further up the road, was a green PMU sign. By the time I'd reached the entrance, a flimsy cover-story had formed in my confused mind.

The place smelled of air-freshener, beer and stale sweat, unfortunately not in that order. A few punters huddled at the counter, watching the first race of the day. *Le Patron* acknowledged me with a nod, then turned to watch the horses and jockeys parading on the TV screen. On a round-topped table, a little way from the bar, sat three glasses of milky-white pastis, a small carafe of water and a No Smoking sign. I heard voices coming from a corridor that led to a covered patio area outside. A squeaky door opened, then banged shut. Someone uttered a curse, and three men barged into the room. Two of them took their seats at the table; the third was already sitting – in his wheelchair.

I had no idea how to introduce myself, and rather than planning my next move I dived straight in.

'*Bonjour, messieurs*,' I said, using my best English accent. 'I'm looking for a gentleman called Le Blaireau?'

The man in the wheelchair flinched and looked up at me with eyes narrowed. Presumably, I neither looked nor sounded like an agent of the fraud squad, and after giving me a quick once-over he relaxed.

'*C'est moi*,' he said, then took a sip of his pastis. I noticed he was wearing a pair of cycling gloves. 'And you are?'

I pulled up a plastic chair and sat down. The other men got up and took their drinks over to the bar.

'Jeanne—' I began, but stopped myself. I put my bag down on the floor, then offered my hand. 'Jean Thompson.'

He gave me a feeble handshake, slicked back his wavy dark hair, stroked his scraggly grey-and-brown beard. There was certainly something of the woodland about him, and his nickname was well chosen. I fought – and lost – the urge to stare at a large mole on his upper lip; it was a beauty.

'*Bonjour*, Madame Thompson. What brings you to Bordeaux?'

'I represent a group of London wine collectors—'

I paused. As bad as my story was, if I didn't rush he might just buy it. 'Do you think I could order a beer?'

Le Blaireau shouted my order to the barman: '*Un demi, Pascal, s'il te plaît.*'

I thanked him, then continued my story. 'I was dining at a restaurant last night, and the maître d'hôtel mentioned that you might have some interesting wine for sale.'

'You work in London, you say?'

I gave him a big smile. 'Yes, I'm based there. I travel all over the world sourcing wines for my clients. We pay upfront and in cash.'

My beer arrived with the bill on a small plastic saucer. Despite a sudden raging thirst, I took only a small sip.

'And someone told you I have something interesting to sell?'

I nodded.

'And did they mention a particular wine?'

'Cheval Blanc '90.'

He took his time, sipped his drink. 'I might have a little in my collection, but a wine like that is very valuable, *madame*.'

'We pay generously for the right wine, even for . . . unprovenanced merchandise.'

He looked hurt. 'What do you mean "unprovenanced"? *madame*, I am a reputable *collectionneur*—'

'I meant no offence,' I said.

With some effort, he removed a leather wallet from his back pocket and took from it a crumpled Polaroid. The way his thigh muscles flexed when he shifted in the seat made me wonder how long he'd been a wheelchair user.

'Here,' he said, passing me the photo, 'You are talking to a hero of La France, *madame*.'

I looked at the faded picture of a man, who bore a slight resemblance to the one in front of me, riding a racing bike along a mountain road.

'I'm impressed, *monsieur*. You were an athlete.'

'Mont Ventoux, almost at the summit.'

The men at the bar sniggered. 'No sign of the other riders, though, Blaireau!' one said. 'They must have left you behind!' said the other.

Le Blaireau's cheeks coloured. 'I was in first place, you idiots. The photo was taken from the lead car!' He looked at me. 'What would they know about cycling? It would take a miracle to get those two layabouts to the top of a mountain!'

The men continued to laugh. 'It would take a miracle for you to buy your friends a drink, Blaireau!'

'What? You think I can afford to pay for your drinks, too? On the meagre disability pension I get from this bloody government? *Ah non*, my friends.' He emptied his glass and sighed. 'No, no, it's the bloody foreigners, the Arabs, the Romas, the Slavs. They get all the state handouts these days, while crippled heroes of La France get left by the wayside. It will take a miracle to change that! A bloody miracle, I tell you!'

His cronies continued to chide him: 'You didn't mind dealing with that Arab the other day though, eh?'

'Business is business, my friends.'

I thought of Hakim Wattar. 'An Arab?' I asked.

'What? Yes, an Arab driving a big German car! What's wrong with a Peugeot or a Renault, eh? Nowadays everyone wants a German car.' He turned to address the others. 'That's the France of today, my friends: a big, hairy Arab driving a brand-new Mercedes with a boot full of Cheval Blanc!'

Big and hairy – he didn't sound like Wattar. But the fact that the man was driving a Mercedes certainly intrigued me. 'So, this was the man who sold you the wine I'm interested in?'

'Yes, but don't worry, *madame*, it is in perfect condition. I have two cases left. To you, five hundred a case, if you take both.'

'Do you have the sales receipts?'

Again he shifted in his wheelchair. 'People don't always keep the paperwork. Many sell their wine before a divorce, or when an elderly parent . . . you know.'

'Can I see the wine?' I asked.

To my surprise, he reached under his wheelchair and pulled out a black sports bag. The bag contained a red-topped wine bottle which, holding it carefully in both gloved hands, he passed to me.

'Château Cheval Blanc '90,' he whispered. 'The rest is in my cellar.'

I examined the label and the red foil capsule. The bottle was filled to the correct level in the neck, and the glass looked authentic – I recognized the maker's mark. My God, I thought, here's my evidence.

'Well, thank you, Monsieur Blaireau. I'll have to speak to a colleague in London this morning and come back to you. May I take this as a sample?'

He smiled. 'No, *madame*, but you will find me here this afternoon if you wish make a purchase.'

I looked again at the bottle I held in my hand. This was crucial evidence that could be the key to solving Rougeard's murder. Somehow I had to take the wine, but how? Maybe I could cause some sort of distraction, spill my drink and make my getaway during the kerfuffle. I played for time, picked up my bag and slung the strap over my shoulder. 'So the Arab drove a Mercedes,' I said, trying to sound casual. 'Was it an expensive one?'

Le Blaireau's smile vanished. 'How should I know, and what's it to you, anyway?'

'Oh, nothing. I was thinking of buying one my-self . . .'

His face darkened. 'Madame Thompson, may I see your business card? You do have one, *non*?'

Oh, bugger, I thought, time to make an exit. 'Er, I've got one in the car,' I lied. 'I'll go and fetch it, if you like.'

'Don't forget to pay for your drink, *madame*. And I will take the wine now, *s'il vous plaît*.'

Reluctantly I handed back the Cheval Blanc. I'd missed my chance.

'*Tenez*,' I called to the barman, placing a five euro note on the plastic saucer. 'I'll be back for my change in two minutes.'

I got up and made my way past the bar towards the exit. Le Blaireau's electric wheelchair whirred behind me.

'Why don't I come with you?' he said. 'I need some fresh air.'

I turned round and looked down at the man. He reached up, put the wine bottle on the counter and grinned at me.

'That will be nice, eh?'

The whirring wheelchair followed me all the way to the door and out into the sunshine. There was no way I was going to give Le Blaireau my business card – the address alone would blow my cover story. I needed to shake him off, pronto. But perhaps now was my chance to make off with the wine. I wondered how fast an electric wheelchair could go. Surely I could outrun one, even in heels.

I turned left on the pavement, walking away from where I'd parked Clémentine. We passed a pharmacy, a boulangerie, an insurance office. He kept pace with me, saying something about how filthy the *quartier* had become. When we reached the corner of the street I stopped abruptly.

'Er . . . goodbye,' I said, turned and sprinted back towards the bar.

'*Putain de salope—*'

At the sound of his shouted curses, everyone on the street stared at us: me, clomping along the pavement in my high heels; Le Blaireau in hot pursuit, his wheelchair motor screaming like a banshee.

I skidded to a halt at the open door of the bar just as the owner poked his head out, curious to see the cause of the commotion. Barging past him, I snatched the Cheval Blanc from the bar. 'Sorry, can't stop! Keep the change!' I shouted, rushing back out and sprinting on towards the car while retrieving the keys from my bag. I could hear Le Blaireau behind me barking orders and insults at the barman, and the whoops of laughter he received by way of reply.

Almost at the car, with the wine clenched under my left armpit, I fumbled for the ignition key and promptly dropped the whole bunch in the gutter. Bending down to retrieve it, I spotted Le Blaireau only twenty-or-so metres away, his gloved hands slapping at the skinny tyres of the chair, propelling him faster and faster towards me. The whirring noise and the shouting were now getting worryingly close.

I tried to unlock the driver's door but the key wouldn't turn; I'd have to use the passenger side. I stepped into the road in the space between Clémentine and the car in front, but in the agonizing moments it took for a heavy goods vehicle to pass by, Le Blaireau had caught up with me.

'Give me back my wine you bitch!' he shouted, swinging his wheelchair round to face the road, its front wheels resting on the edge of the kerb.

A gap in the traffic allowed me to reach the passenger door, but what I saw next stopped me dead. Le Blaireau, after glancing left and right, rose to his feet and stumbled towards me. Instinctively, I moved towards the back of the car. Still muttering curses and fixing me with murderous eyes, Le Blaireau chased me twice round the car – first one way, then the other. God knows what he would do if he caught me, but I wasn't keen to find out. This bizarre game of cat and mouse continued until I gained enough ground to unlock the door and jump in. I clicked the lock, shuffled across bench seat to the driver's side and started the engine. Le Blaireau, red in the face and thumping the bonnet with both fists, looked like he was about to have a heart attack. My own heart felt like it was about to burst. I reversed a couple of feet, then moved forward, turning into the traffic, hopeful a kind-hearted driver would let me out. A white delivery van slowed and Le Blaireau, breathless and defeated, stood to the side to avoid a tangle with Clémentine's front bumper as I pulled out.

Less than a hundred metres ahead a stationary queue of traffic had blocked the road, so I made a u-turn and doubled back, wheels spinning. I raced back towards Le Blaireau who, by now, had positioned himself in the middle of the road. He jumped out of the way as I sped past, then jogged after me, shouting curses and shaking his fist. When I reached the junction with the main road he has still visible, hopping about and gesticulating. All this talk of miracles, I thought, and then you see one right there in the rear-view mirror!

I'd forgotten about Lefèvre's clumsy, hurtful comments. Why should I care about his feelings for me? I was proud of my private detective work and delighted to have discovered something he didn't know. Clémentine's skinny tyres were carrying me home, racing along the left bank of the Garonne. My heart was racing too, as I considered the possible links between Rougeard's killer, the wine stolen from his cellar, and the badger in the wheelchair.

I crossed the Mitterrand Bridge, humming the tune to *A Case of You*. It's funny, but try as I might, I couldn't get Lefèvre out of my head, or stop thinking about that kiss after the opera.

That brief, ambiguous little kiss.

I was blissfully happy, on a high. And when you're on a high, you never think about the lows that are bound to follow.

In my haste to leave the city, I'd also forgotten Wendy's newspaper.

Twelve-fifteen in Libourne. A sudden rainstorm and the lunchtime exodus had emptied the streets. I parked up and hurried to the *maison de la presse* on Rue Gambetta before it closed for lunch, dodging puddles and trying not to slip on the shiny wet cobbles. After buying Wendy's *Guardian*, I couldn't resist the delicious aromas of baking coming from Patisserie Lopez opposite. I can never pass this shop without buying something.

Clutching a paper bag full of macaroons and *bouchons de Bordeaux*, and holding the newspaper over my head, I made it back to the car just as a rain shower became a downpour.

I opened the paper and spread out the pages to dry on the bench seat beside me. A photograph of the Libyan president stared back at me under the headline 'GADAFFI VOWS TO STAY'. The man's height and bulk, dark curls, moustache and wispy beard reminded me of Le Blaireau's description of 'the big hairy Arab'. I thought, too, of Hakim Wattar's jinn and the white-clad intruder in my dream.

I had no working hypothesis, merely a fanciful scenario that went like this: a big, strong North-African had broken into René Rougard's to steal his expensive wine collection. Something went wrong, and the burglar killed Rougeard then tried to frame Hakim Wattar for the crime. Some of the wine taken from Lacasse was planted at Wattar's place, and the rest sold to Le Blaireau in Bordeaux.

Several things bothered me: if the Cheval Blanc was genuine, how had Rougeard invested in such expensive wine? How could he afford to run a top-of-the-range Mercedes? And how had he rescued his business from bankruptcy to become a high-rolling gambler at the casino? If the wine was fake, was he perhaps involved in some sort of counterfeiting scam?

Perhaps Lemaitre, the casino owner, was right: Rougeard had simply been enjoying a lucky streak. Somehow I didn't believe it.

I needed to talk to somebody; Lefèvre was out of the question, so I decided to go and see John Clare.

Domaine du Soleil was living up to its name. The morning's showers had gone and the sun shone over Claire's vineyards. The vines were in great shape, heavy with almost-ripe bunches of merlot grapes. In the daylight, the outside of the building looked every bit as cosseted as its interior. The house, winery and stables enclosed an immaculate white gravel courtyard on three sides. Virginia creeper scaled the ancient stone walls, and a topiary hedge formed the boundary on the fourth side of the court. An archway, cut into the hedge, joined the courtyard to a sea of vines and, beyond them, hundreds of hectares of forest.

John Clare's Range Rover was absent. His dogs, if they were at home, were silent. No one came to the door when I rang the bell.

Oh, well, I thought, nobody home.

I got back in the car, made a three-point turn and took a final glance in the wing mirror before driving off. In one of the first-floor windows a curtain twitched and a hand, parting the heavy fabric, retreated into the blackness of the room.

Mention Bordeaux, and most people think of fine and rare wines. But here's the irony: the bulk of Bordeaux's produce is neither rare nor remarkably fine. Every year, nearly six million hectolitres of wine bear the Bordeaux name, enough – so they say – to fill two hundred Olympic swimming pools. Nor does much of it come from Bordeaux itself. The best stuff is made in rural villages like Margaux and Pauillac in the Médoc, and Pomerol and Saint-Emilion near Libourne. But most of Bordeaux's ordinary plonk is made in anonymous, out-of-the-way places, a long way from the city – places like Les Eglisottes. The town, barely more than a high street with a bar, a bank and two bakeries, has a hair salon and a florist in the square next to the church, and a funeral business a little way out along the Coutras road. It's the kind of place where farmers drive their tractors into town to buy cigarettes; where elderly ladies park outside the shops and leave their engines running; where the traffic stops to allow mangy cats to cross the road; and where everybody knows everybody's business and nothing out of the ordinary goes unnoticed.

And no one gets murdered and dumped in a vat of wine – until last Sunday, that is.

God, it was hot when I arrived outside the Bar des Sports. I'd opened the ventilation flaps in Clémentine's dashboard and flipped up the windows, but the dark clouds in the west that threatened further showers meant the cloth roof would have to stay on for now. Having eaten half the goodies from Patisserie Lopez, I was thirsty. A cup of tea at John Clare's would have been just the ticket. After the encounter with Le Blaireau my nerves were on edge, and witnessing the mysterious hand at Clare's window hadn't helped. I suppose I needed a drink in more ways than one.

The bar was owned by a chubby, friendly-faced man in his late forties. I ordered a Perrier and a glass of *vin blanc* – the one for my thirst, the other for my nerves. He offered me a table outside and we chatted about the weather, the grape harvest, winter hunting in the forest. I liked the way his lips curved naturally into a smile after each puff on his cigarette. He reminded me of a smiley, overweight Serge Gainsbourg, and I think he took me for a British tourist on a late summer break – until, that is, I asked about the recent murder.

'Oh, *mon dieu*,' he said, 'you heard about that? Yes, the dead man was here in my bar when he was last seen.'

'But I thought he was arrested and taken to the *gendarmerie* after the fight?'

'Yes, but he was here in my bar when he was last seen in Les Eglisottes.' Proud of this detail, he flicked the ash from his Gitanne and smiled at me again, wagging his finger. 'I think you are not a holidaymaker, *madame*. You have a house here? In the Dordogne, *peut-être*?'

'No, I live in Saint-Emilion.'

He looked surprised.

'I'm a winemaker,' I explained.

'*Une vigneronne Anglaise*,' he said, the conversation slipping into French, 'well I shouldn't be surprised. Most of the vineyard workers are Romanians or Algerians now – why not an English winemaker!'

'I make very good wine, *monsieur*,' I said.

He looked at me, took another puff.

'Talent and beauty often go together, *madame*. I'm sure your wine is very good indeed.'

He laughed, his cheeks flushed, and he retreated indoors promising to bring me a refill. Must be from the Corrèze, I thought. Like my late husband, Olivier, and his father, the Correzians I'd known had all been inveterate flatterers.

When he returned, carrying a small jug of white wine,

I asked him about the fight between Rougeard and the Algerian.

He sat down opposite me. 'On the house, okay?' he said, topping up my glass.

'Oh, thank you. I read all about it in *Le Sud Ouest*.'

'Ah, but let me tell you what the papers couldn't print, eh?'

I was intrigued. 'Please do.'

'Well, you know they arrested two local men? An Algerian boy and the Englishman who lives next to the Rougeard place.'

'John Clare?'

'You know him? Ah, of course, another English winemaker. He's a nice guy. I like him. I don't care what people say – live and let live, that's my motto.

'Anyway, I've never had any trouble with either of them – well, not until last week. The Algerian boy likes to drink, you see, and it had been such a hot day. He was on his second bottle when Rougeard came in and accused him of stealing.'

'So, he was a thief?'

'I don't know – the story goes that Rougeard owed him money. Perhaps he had just taken what was owed to him. Anyway, this is what happened next. The boy denied it and told Rougeard to go and boil his head. Rougeard called him a filthy Arab who didn't even follow his own heathen scriptures. That made the boy mad. Then he called Wattar a *pédé,* said he was leading a sinful life with the Englishman. That made him even madder. Then, paff! the kid threw a punch at Rougeard, got him right on the jaw. I phoned the *gendarmerie* straight away. Luckily there were a few of us here to keep them apart while we waited for the *flics* to arrive.'

He took a breath, stubbed out his cigarette. 'Like I say, it's all the same to me – blacks, Muslims, gays – as long as my customers pay their bills and don't break anything, they're welcome.'

'So do you get a lot of North Africans here?'

'Not many! They're not supposed to drink, you know. Apart from Wattar, there's only one I remember – the police thought they might know each other but I don't think Wattar even noticed the man.'

'Now you've lost me,' I said.

'He was here, the night of the fight.'

Interesting, I thought. 'An Algerian, like Wattar?'

'I don't know, a big North African. He ordered a Coca Zero and sat quietly in the corner throughout the whole thing. Thankfully he didn't get involved – I don't think we could have restrained him as easily as the other two. He left after they'd taken Hakim and Rougeard away.'

'You never saw him again?'

'*Ah, non.*'

'And he was big, you say?'

'Yes – tall, muscular, long hair . . . one of those little beards, you know.'

'Did he say anything to you?'

'Not much. Only—' He paused, scratching his stubbly chin. 'When he paid his bill I was apologetic, you know, for the upset. Then he said "He too will pay."'

'And you told this to the *gendarmes*?'

'Of course. They wrote it all down.'

I settled my bill, left a generous tip and walked over to the car park at the side of the bar.

'Nice car!' he called after me.

Unlocking the driver's door, I heard the roar of a powerful engine as a big burgundy 4x4 pulled up in the parking space next to me.

'I thought it was you.' I recognised the driver's voice and his car.

'Hello there,' I said to John Clare as he jumped out of the Range Rover.

We double kissed in the awkward way the English do.

'I love the car.'

'You too? She's called Clémentine,' I said proudly.

78

'Great name. So, what are you doing in Les Eglisottes?'

'I came to see you. I went to the house, but . . . there was nobody there.'

He pointed to the back of the car where the two Dobermans sat panting at the rear window. 'Just been to the vets to get Priscilla and Dorothy their annual jabs.' He reached inside and buzzed the windows down. 'Fancy a drink?'

'I've just had one, John, but yes, why not?'

We walked over to the table I'd only just vacated. John and the bar owner shook hands like old friends, asked after each other's health. John ordered a beer; I stuck to Perrier.

'Is there someone in the house, John?' I asked, after the small talk was over.

'Yes. Why?'

'Oh, it's just that when I called round earlier, I saw somebody, at the window upstairs.'

'That'll be Hakim. Hope he didn't scare you.'

'No, not at all. So, they released him, then?'

'Lack of evidence. Rougeard's fingerprints and Hakim's were on the bottles, but that's all they had.'

'How is he?'

'He's okay, but he won't answer the door. He's still very shaken by what happened.'

'I can imagine,' I said, taking a sip of the fizzy mineral water.

We both acknowledged a greeting from an elderly lady passing by.

'So, why did you come to see me?' he asked.

Where to start? My theory about the wine theft gone wrong? The nameless, faceless 'big Arab' whom I suspected of committing the crime? The farce with Le Blaireau that morning? In the end I replied to John's question with a one of my own. 'What do you make of Captain Lefèvre?'

John swigged his beer, looking at me over the rim of

his glass, eyes twinkling. 'You like him, don't you?'

'We're friends, I suppose – well, I thought we were.'

'Okay, so I can't really badmouth him then, can I?'

'And would you?'

He put down his glass and sighed.

'Actually, I think he's alright. Quite tasty in fact.'

'Hands off. I saw him first.'

'No, seriously, he's okay. He was almost apologetic when he let Hakim go yesterday. He asked after you, too.'

'What did he say?'

'Said would I pass on my regards if I saw you.'

'Regards?'

'Well . . . that's not a bad start, Jeanne. I think he likes you too.'

This was silly. I felt like a teenage girl, gossiping about a boy I had a crush on, while what I'd really come to talk to John about was far more serious than my interest in Lefèvre.

'Well,' I said, 'he's going a funny way about it.'

John's eyebrows lifted. 'Do tell.'

By the time I'd finished relating the incident in the police squad room, *le patron* had replenished our drinks, and John Clare was gazing at me, smiling.

'Sounds to me like he's too embarrassed to say anything. He's single, you say; was he ever married?'

I gave John a précised account of Lefèvre's personal tragedy.

'Well, then,' he said, 'maybe your captain's just too scared to open up, you know, reluctant to express his true feelings in case he gets hurt again.'

'You should write an advice column.'

'Just call me Aunty John.'

We both smiled. John Clare showed all the signs of becoming a good friend. We watched another passerby – this time an old man dragging a reluctant dachshund along on one of those extendable leads.

'Actually,' he continued, 'I used to be a journalist.'

'Oh, really?'

'Yeah, on a couple of nationals.'

'Gosh, how fascinating. What on earth made you give up your career to come and live in the sticks?

'A mixture of impulsive madness and love – probably one and the same thing when you think about it.'

'I know what you mean.'

'You, too?'

'Yep,' I sighed. He didn't ask me to explain and I didn't want to. Instead I told him my hunch that the man who'd killed Rougeard had also framed Hakim Wattar. He let me ramble on about the other things: the spooky figure I'd seen at the casino, my encounter with the badger in the wheelchair, even my eerie nightmare and the owl that had scared me half to death.

After a quarter of an hour our glasses were empty.

I wondered whether John was getting tired of the conversation. 'Sorry,' I said. 'I'm boring you.'

'Of course not.'

'No, I shouldn't burden you with all this stuff. You and Hakim must have had enough of—'

'Look, Jeanne,' John said, slipping a bank note on the table and securing it with a handful of change, 'you've got to tell the police all this, especially about the wheelchair guy.'

I must have looked unconvinced.

'Seriously, Jeanne, go and see Lefèvre. You never know, he might just declare his love for you.'

'I doubt it,' I said, hoping, desperately hoping, he was right. We strolled back to our cars.

'Thanks, Aunty,' I said.

'Don't mention it. By the way, where did you meet him – the captain?'

'Oh, now that *is* a long story, John. How long have you got?'

'I'm a good listener.'

I leaned against Clémentine's front wing. 'Come to supper tonight and I'll tell you.'

'I'd love to, but I'm not sure I can leave Hakim on his

own.'

Brushing aside any fears about the mysterious hand at the curtains, I said, 'Bring him along too, if you like.'

'I'll ask him'

'Great. See you at eight-ish?'

'Okay.'

'Here,' I said, taking a business card from my bag. 'This is me: Château Fontloube, half way up the côte, just off the D245.'

'Hello, John. You're on your own, then?'

John trotted up the stone steps to the front door carrying a bunch of roses and a small paper-wrapped parcel. 'Hakim's happy to stay at home with the dogs. Here, these are for you.'

I accepted the flowers. 'Thank you, John. Still, pity he couldn't make it.'

I led him through the house and out onto the patio. Gathered round the table were Archie and Loubna at one end and Wendy at the other, mixing herself a glass of *kir*.

'Ah, there you are,' Wendy trilled.

'This is John everyone,' I said. 'John, this is my good friend Wendy, that's Archie, and that's Loubna, who helped Hakim at the police station.'

John double kissed the ladies, shook hands with Archie.

'My dear boy,' Wendy said, handing John a glass, and fixing him with an adoring stare, 'what a handsome fellow you are! And a famous journalist to boot, so Jeanne tells me.'

'I . . . thank you. I wouldn't say famous. Lovely to meet you, Wendy.'

'Don't go smothering him, Wendy,' I said, taking my own glass to make a toast. Turk emerged from under the table, his stumpy tail wagging, and gave us a friendly woof. 'Oh, and that's Turk. Now, here's to new friends and a successful harvest. *À nous!*'

We all chinked glasses.

Loubna offered round a platter of ripe figs stuffed with goat's cheese. When she got to John she asked, 'How is Monsieur Wattar?'

'He's fine, thank you. Mmm, these look delicious. He asked me to give you this.'

Loubna put down the figs, took a parcel from John and carefully removed the wrapping. Inside was a small book.

'*Le Prophète,*' she said, reading the book's title. 'What a thoughtful gift. Please pass on my thanks to your friend.'

'I will,' John said, turning to Wendy whose gaze had remained fixed on him. 'Have you tried a fig, Wendy?'

'No, dear, the seeds get stuck under my dental plate.'

No one can say whether Archie's extraordinary mental powers gave him his acute sense of smell. But he does have a truly gifted nose – a nose that can identify hundreds of different aromas. On three occasions he has won first prize in blind tasting competitions, much to the amazement of the other competitors – usually older, far more experienced wine experts than himself. He says it's all down to two things: focus and recall. Having Aspergers helps him focus on the subject, mentally cataloguing the countless smells contained in wine; and his synaesthesia allows him to sense each nuance visually – in his mind's eye, you might say. I'm rightly proud of my in-house oenologist, and no visit to Fontloube is complete without a demonstration of his skills.

After our aperitifs, I gave John a quick tour of the vines and the winery, then Archie and I took him downstairs for a taste of last year's vintage. The château's vaulted cellars, hewn from the limestone rock of the côte, contain thousands of bottles of Château Fontloube and a hundred-or-so oak barrels called *barriques.*

My father-in-law, Henri, who planted many of the vines still growing on Fontloube's slopes, was a tidy man. He kept a tidy cellar and a tidy vineyard. He taught me his system for sorting and fermenting the grape crop, a tradition that continues to this day. We divide the vineyard into sections called parcels. Each parcel contains vines of a particular grape variety and age. Some parcels are planted on the light, limestone-rich soils of the côte, while others are located in the flatter, more gravelly loams towards the plain. Old vines, that Henri planted over fifty years ago, grow in separate parcels from those planted more recently. In the winter following the harvest, the wine is put into barriques where it matures for a year or so. Scribbled in chalk on the end of each barrique is a number identifying the wine's original parcel.

I drew a pipette-full of wine from a barrel of old-vine merlot and filled three glasses. John put his nose in the glass and sniffed. We watched him intently, curious to hear his judgement.

'Mmm, ripe, rich . . . older vines? . . . lovely plummy fruit . . .'

John proved to be a competent taster. This year would be his fifth harvest, and he clearly knew his stuff. We tasted the merlots and the cabernets, the old and the young vines. I handed John the glass pipette and asked him to choose a barrel at random and draw a glassful for Archie.

John went into an adjacent vault and returned a few moments later. He passed a glass to Archie who raised it to his nose, closed his eyes and inhaled.

'Green-gold and silver,' Archie said. 'Parcel number eighteen, halfway up the côte, young cabernets.'

'Wow, spot on,' John said, looking at me. I invited him to try another, and he scuttled off again with the pipette. This time Archie pronounced it to be a 'shimmering purple-silver' from parcel number five. Again, John looked amazed.

He made Archie identify a good half dozen different barrels before declaring that there was no point trying to catch the boy out – he was, quite simply, a genius. 'I'd be fascinated to know what you think of my wine, Archie,' he said. 'Can I send you a bottle?' Archie gathered up the glasses. 'If you like,' he said, shaking the dregs into the drain.

'Come on, chaps,' I said, 'let's go and eat.'

An alfresco supper, a golden sunset to set the vines aglow, a bottle or two of wine shared between friends: what better way to end a nerve-wracking day? We'd finished the main course, Archie and Loubna had gone for a stroll in the vineyard, and I still hadn't told John how I met Pierre Lefèvre. We'd started on the cheese before he reminded me of my promise.

'So, come on,' he said, 'tell me how you met the handsome police captain.'

Wendy gave me a sympathetic smile, then went indoors to fetch another bottle. I hate talking about myself. Playing for time, I smeared a pungent slice of camembert onto a chunk of bread, but John was insistent. 'Go on, where did you find him?'

'Well, like I said, it's a long story.'

'I'm listening.'

'Okay. Well, the very first time we met I was in my twenties – he was investigating my late husband's accident. Then, more recently, our paths crossed again. A couple of years ago, a young student apprentice called Aimée came to stay at Fontloube. We found out later that she – well, she had quite a history. She got involved with a drug dealer, stole my 4x4 and some money.'

'Good grief, where did you find her?'

'She found us, really. She and Andrew – that's Archie's dad – knew each other before I met him. And, to cut a long, sad story short, she was killed. Death by misadventure was the coroner's verdict.'

'Oh my God, Jeanne, what happened?'

'She was living in Bordeaux by then. I think – no, I *know* – she was murdered. Turk and I went to look for her associates, didn't we, boy?' I scratched Turk behind the ear, ruffled his fur. 'Lefèvre arrested the whole gang.'

John looked at me, suddenly concerned, hutched his chair up closer to mine and put his arm round my shoulder. I was crying.

'Oh, I'm sorry, John.' I said.

'No, Jeanne, I'm sorry. I shouldn't have forced you to tell me. It must have been a terrible experience.'

I felt silly, mainly because John didn't know the half of it. I took a deep breath. 'No, it's not just that, John. You see, Andrew and I were only together for eighteen months. He died the Christmas before last – cancer.' I dried my eyes, blew my nose. 'Then the man responsible for Aimée's death kidnapped me and I got shot. Luckily, Lefèvre came to my rescue, and so here I am.'

Now he looked more shocked than concerned; people always do. That's why I don't like talking about myself.

'Since then, Lefèvre has been very supportive, very kind – until this week, that is.'

'Oh, Jeanne, I had no idea. But you have to talk to him about what happened today. And you mustn't go putting yourself at risk again.'

'Yes,' I said, looking at my morsel of cheese, 'I know.'

Vendredi 9 Séptembre 2011

My eyes opened to a bright, sunny morning, but behind them gathered the dark clouds of a hangover. I'd drunk too much wine at dinner last night – and after dinner, too, truth be told. To begin with, the evening had been such fun: new friends enjoying a late-summer supper in the cool of the vineyard; Archie's blind tasting in the cellars; Loubna's delicious lamb tajine; my account of the incident with The Badger – 'what larks!' Wendy had said. But then things started to go downhill. At what point did the mood change? John's words, *you shouldn't put yourself at risk*, echoed round my alcohol-addled mind. That was the conversation, the release point, that triggered my free-fall into the gloom. Now, as well as the familiar feeling of melancholy, I had the mother of all headaches too. I was also more than usually anxious about something. What was it I had to do?

Then it came to me: the ceremony was only a week away, and I had an appointment at the town hall at eleven o'clock to collect my robes. Oh well, I thought, at least it would take my mind off the hangover. Without my rendezvous at the town hall and the million-and-one other things I had to prepare for the harvest, I'd have stayed in bed all morning. Thankfully the appointment would drag me back to the real world, and for the moment, I could put the black thoughts to one side. I still had to confront my headache and the growing queasiness in my stomach, so I went downstairs in search of coffee and pain killers.

Two other anxieties bothered me as I drank the coffee

– one almost spiritual, the other corporeal. I've never been much of a churchgoer, but I got married in the church at Saint-Emilion, and I buried two men there: my late husband, Olivier, and his father, Henri. Every July on their saints' days I visit the collegiate church to light a candle in their memory. This summer, however, I'd forgotten, and something was nagging me to do it now. The other concern I had was about my weight. Wendy says I'm a curvy size 12, bless her, but since the hard work of last winter I'd put on a few pounds, and I wondered if Pierre might think I was, well, you know . . . So, with my conscience tugging at both sleeves, lacking in faith and a little out of shape, I decided to ride my bicycle to church before collecting my robes.

And what was the other thing? What else had John said to me? Ah, yes: speak to Lefèvre.

I'd arrived at the collegiate church at ten-thirty, but hadn't been able to go in. The rows of cars parked on both sides of the Avenue Verdun confirmed what the chiming bells had suggested: a funeral was taking place. Candles for Olivier and Henri would have to wait. After getting my breath back, gazing at the west door's carved stone tympanum, I'd decided to pedal round the corner to the Tour du Roi where, a week on Sunday, the Jurade's harvest ceremony would reach its climax.

I was standing on the parapet of the tower, looking down on the rooftops and, beyond, to Saint-Emilion's southern vineyards – a thousand hectares of nearly ripe grapes soaking up the September sunshine. Vines need sunshine, but they also need rain. Too much rain though, especially during the harvest, dilutes the juice and makes a thin wine. Not enough sunshine, and the fruit won't ripen; the wine will be aggressive and sharp. In just over a week's time I'd be here with my fellow initiates to proclaim the year's harvest – a successful harvest, I hoped, but one that depended on the weather remaining fine and dry. If the rains returned, however, this year's vintage could be a disaster.

Lefèvre, I reasoned, was juggling with different but no less troubling factors. What had he said in the squad room? *A few clues and not enough evidence.* Evidence, I imagined, was a detective's stock-in-trade. Evidence was what I had to offer, but I wasn't going to deliver it to Lefèvre's door; if he wanted it, he'd have to come to me. There was no way I was going back to that squad room.

I rummaged in my bag for the phone, dialled his number.

'Are you alright, Jeanne,' he said, softly.

'Yes, thank you. I have an appointment at the *mairie* at eleven, so I'm killing time.'

'Okay . . .' He paused, and I held my tongue. 'Would you like to meet up?'

'I don't know, Pierre.'

Again, silence. Again, I waited.

'Listen, Jeanne, I am really sorry for the misunderstanding.'

Oh God, I thought, why does he sound so bloody contrite? In spite of the paracetamols I'd taken, my vital organs were in turmoil. My stomach wanted to know why I'd skipped breakfast; my brain was ordering me to stay calm; my feet, as usual, grumbled about their working conditions. My poor, piteous heart whispered, *forgive him.*

I sighed. 'Okay, Pierre, let's forget about it. I have some information for you about the wine stolen from Rougeard's. Well, actually I have another bottle of the stuff.'

'Jeanne, where are you?'

'In Saint-Emilion, the King's Tower.'

'I'll be there right away.'

I was still standing on the parapet ten minutes later when I heard Pierre's voice.

'Don't jump!'

I looked down at the terrace, a hundred feet below

me, and saw his upturned face, eyes shaded by his right hand. A brief moment of vertigo made me step back from the edge.

'Don't flatter yourself, Pierre. You didn't upset me that much.'

'*Quoi?* I'll come up. Wait there!'

I'd been at the edge of life's parapet once, many years ago, after my third and final miscarriage. I know what it's like to be tempted by suicide, when the fear of death is trumped by the pain of living. Since then I've learned how to deal with such temptations. Nowadays, surrounded by the people who rely on me and on whom I rely, I get along okay.

Pierre appeared, slightly out of puff, with an empty evidence bag and a smile.

We double air-kissed.

'I had no idea there were so many steps,' he said. 'What were you saying? I couldn't hear you.'

'Never, mind. Listen, I went to Bordeaux yesterday, to a bar in Bègles, and got this . . .'

I reached into my bag and took out the Cheval Blanc, which I'd covered in bubble wrap. Pierre pursed his lips and exhaled.

'Got?'

'Well, I took it from a man in a wheelchair called The Badger. He deals in dodgy wine from the bar PMU.'

Pierre took the bottle, held it at arm's length, and scrutinised the label.

The smile faded. 'You mean you *stole* it?'

'Pierre, this is evidence. I think it's from the same batch stolen from Rougeard's place. This Badger fellow told me he received it from a big hairy Arab. He's selling the stuff for only fifty euros a bottle – it can't be legitimate.'

'Jeanne, I've told you before not to put yourself in danger. Is there any point in repeating myself again?'

'No, because I wasn't in danger.'

'Did you go with anyone?'

'No, I didn't need to—'

'You go alone to a Bordeaux *banlieue* to meet a man whom you believe to be a criminal? Don't you think that is a little . . . risky?'

I thought about it. He did have a point.

'I'm impulsive, Pierre. You know that.'

'Okay,' he said, sighing, returning his attention to the wine bottle, 'but let me know before you go crusading again.'

'I will. Now, what do make of that?'

'Looks like the same wine: Château Cheval Blanc 1990. Could be a coincidence . . . there must be millions of bottles, *non?*'

'Only a hundred-and-eighty thousand that year – I looked it up. Half of it was exported, and the rest sold for a small fortune to rich collectors, high-end restaurants and five-star hotels.'

'How much is a small fortune?'

'I don't know, two, three hundred a bottle, at least.'

'Not the sort of wine that changes hands for fifty euros, then?'

'No.'

'Unless it was counterfeit?'

'. . . which is what I thought at first, but it looks genuine to me.'

'This is not my area of expertise, Jeanne—'

'The nearest *laboratoire* is in Bergerac. You could send it for analysis—' I was interrupted by the first of eleven chimes ringing out over the rooftops. 'Oops, must go or I'll be late for my fitting.'

'Ah, yes, your induction into the Jurade! Lamarque told me – you know he's a senior member. I'm sure you will look very charming in your robes.'

Charming? What did he mean by that? Charming enticing? Charming sophisticated? Charming middle-aged woman in a frumpy medieval gown? I put one hand on my hip, fiddling with a rogue tress of hair. 'Well, perhaps you should ask Commissaire Lamarque for an invitation.'

His smile returned. 'I imagine that Madame Lamarque will be his guest.'

Go on, Jeanne, go on, I said to myself. 'Well . . . perhaps, if you get that wine analysed, and tell me how grateful you are to me for helping you, I might invite you as *my* guest.'

He took a step closer to me, put his hand on the tower's ancient stonework.

'Jeanne, it would be a great honour and an immense pleasure.'

'So?'

'Okay, we will see if this is Rougeard's wine, and interview this wheelchair guy if necessary. And, thank you.'

'It's a date.' I kissed him on both cheeks. 'By the way, be careful of The Badger. He's a fake. There's nothing wrong with his legs.'

Before Pierre could further admonish me I ducked under his arm and flew down the one hundred stone steps to retrieve my bike.

I arrived at the town hall and stopped next to a posh silver Mercedes sporting a devil logo on its number plate. Jogging up the steps to the main door, I bumped into Victor Lemaitre – literally. He was carrying a suit bag and wearing pointy grey shoes, a shiny blue suit and a scarlet felt hat. The hat and the location sparked a memory, and I recalled where I'd seen Lemaitre before our meeting at the Casino. We'd both been here at the town hall a couple of months earlier to attend a meeting of the Jurade's initiates.

'*Pardonnez-moi* – oh, it is you! Madame . . . ?'

'Valeix,' I said, 'Nice to see you again Monsieur Lemaitre.'

'Likewise, Madame Valeix.'

I stared incredulously at the hat, trying hard not to giggle. 'Here to try on your robes, eh? I think you may have forgotten something . . .'

He raised a pudgy hand and swiped the incongruous

item from his head. His face went the same colour as the hat. As I say, if you didn't pity them . . .

'Ah, yes, I suppose I did.' He cleared his throat. 'How do you know the reason for my visit?'

'Apart from the hat? Well, I told you – we have met before.'

He shrugged. 'I'm sorry, I don't follow . . .'

'It was here, for the Jurade meeting in July.'

The light dawned. '*Putain*! Of course! I'm sorry I didn't recognise you at the Casino. Yes, you arrived late and sat at the back.'

'That was me.'

'Ah, so we are to be honoured by the brotherhood together!'

'Looks like it,' I said. 'What's your nomination for – slot machines or cars?'

'You underestimate me, Madame Valeix. I am also the owner of La Girondine – perhaps you have heard of it?'

Such sarcasm! Of course I'd heard of it. S.A.S. La Girondine was a major wine broker in the region, trading in millions of litres of wine. They bought wine in bulk at a low price and sold most of what they bottled overseas. 'Here, take this,' he said, passing me his business card. 'If ever you are looking for a buyer . . .'

'Thanks,' I said, reaching into my bag to find my own crumpled card. 'This is my place – Château Fontloube, between the côte and the railway line. You can't miss it – there's usually a bright orange 2CV on the drive.'

He took the card.

'Thank you,' he said, lingering on the steps. 'By the way, how's our friend Pierre Lefèvre getting on with that dreadful murder? I heard they arrested an Arab?'

'An Algerian, yes,' I said, but didn't elaborate. 'That's all I know.'

'Indeed. So, until Sunday week, then?'

'Yes, until then.'

He took a few paces towards his car, then turned

round. 'I look forward to seeing you in your ceremonial robes. I'm sure you will look divine!'

Creep, I thought.

'*Au revoir*, Monsieur Lemaitre.'

'*Au revoir.*'

In the space of a week three men – Victor Lemaitre, Xavier Foliot and Pierre Lefèvre – had commented on my looks in more-or-less positive terms. But although I'd gladly trade a thousand praises from the first two for one heartfelt compliment from Pierre, his had been the least complimentary. *Charming.* And I had to concede that, of the three, Pierre's remark was probably the most sincere. Did I really imagine that, at forty-six, I could still stir a man's passions? Well, I could hope.

I stood before a full-length mirror in an empty meeting room feeling, frankly, silly. Here was Jeanne Valeix, née Thompson, dressed as a medieval burgher in scarlet robe, pleated jabot and white cape, white gloves and a red *toque* atop her wind-worried chestnut hair; still wearing, beneath the finery, a pair of tight denim shorts and a rough cotton blouse. My reflexion seemed to accuse me of something I had always known: I was an imposter, a fake. The student lawyer from Cheltenham who'd run away to the Bordeaux wine lands was now supposed to be one of Saint-Emilion's movers and shakers. So why was it I still felt more like Miss Thompson than Madame Valeix? Strange, I mused, how things change, and how so much stays the same. I took a step closer to the mirror and examined my face. What did Pierre Lefèvre see when he looked into these eyes? Did he know how much I liked him? Did *I* even know? I slipped out of the red robe, took off the hat and gloves, and imagined Pierre with me, here, now, willing me, helping me, to take off the rest.

I stuffed the smaller items in my bag, folded the gown to fit in my bicycle's wicker basket and left, somewhat red in the face.

I freewheeled downhill, along the côte that leads back to Fontloube, enjoying the rush of cool air caressing my chest and bare arms. The rough tarmac rumbled under the bike's skinny tyres, and I adopted a prone posture, picturing myself as a rider in the Tour de France. My crotch brushed against the leather seat producing a pleasant tingling sensation. While gravity carried me towards home, faster and faster, another fantasy formed in my distracted mind – another fantasy involving Pierre Lefèvre. I imagined the two of us together in a variety of erotic scenarios: in my bed at Fontloube; on the back seat of his unmarked police car; in a moment of utter abandon beneath the vines . . . What was I thinking, fantasising like a teenager? Still, the fantasy and the feeling between my legs were very enjoyable. I coasted the last hundred metres towards the château and arrived at the gate just as Wendy was emptying the letterbox.

'Hi, Wendy,' I panted. 'Anything interesting?'

'Oh, the usual . . .' She looked me up and down. 'Why are you so hot and flustered?'

I considered the question. 'I guess I'm a bit out of shape.'

She narrowed her eyes, squinting into the sun. 'Hard work is it, pedalling downhill?'

'Oh, it's probably the heat.'

'Or the menopause, my dear. I remember when I went through "the change" – it was around the time the Berlin wall came down.'

Cheeky moo, I thought. 'Was it traumatic?'

'No, dear, the Germans were delighted.'

'You know what I mean!'

'Oh, I can't remember. It's such a long time ago. Hot flushes are now a thing of the past for me, I'm pleased to say.' She passed me the letters, flashed me a wry smile. 'Except when one has . . . impure thoughts.'

'Wendy! I'm shocked.'

She laughed. 'Oh don't judge me too harshly, my gorgeous girl. Thoughts are all I have now.'

I got off the bike. 'I know what you mean,' I sighed.

Wendy closed the letterbox door and locked it. 'Don't be ridiculous, Jeanne. You are beautiful young woman. And I'm sure that, when the moment arrives, your captain will fully appreciate it.'

Over the years I have come to realize that Wendy has the uncanny ability to read my mind.

Samedi 10 Séptembre 2011

Putting my makeup on in the bedroom, I heard Wendy call to me from the foot of the stairs. 'Halloo! Jeanne! Telephone!'

I snapped shut the lid of my powder compact, and snapped out of yet another daydream about Lefèvre. With one last pout in the dressing table mirror, I dabbed both wrists with No.5 and then trotted downstairs to where Wendy stood waiting for me.

'It's the captain,' she whispered, passing me the phone.

'*Allo?*'

'*Bonjour,* Jeanne, this is Pierre. I tried your mobile a few times, but . . .'

'Hello, Pierre. Yes, sorry, the battery's flat – you know what I'm like with mobile phones.'

'Yes, I remember you nearly got killed once because—'

'Okay, Pierre, don't lecture me. I'll charge it up right away.'

'Good. Listen, I'm calling to let you know we brought The Badger in first thing this morning. He denies everything, says he was in Arcachon on Monday, doesn't remember ever meeting you or receiving any stolen wine.'

'And do you believe him?'

'No, not one bit, but we've got nothing on him – the bottle's clean, the only fingerprints on it are yours. We had to let him go, so do be careful, okay? And keep your phone with you.'

'Okay,' I said.

'Jeanne,' he said, exhaling. 'We have rearrested Hakim Wattar.'

'What!?'

'We had to, Jeanne. Foliot ordered another search of Wattar's apartment and the boys discovered something that ties him to the crime.'

I was incredulous. 'What's that?'

'Forgive me, Jeanne, but I can't disclose—'

'Never mind, Pierre, I'm coming to the station.'

'Jeanne, it's not—'

I slammed down the phone and grabbed the car keys. There was no way Hakim had murdered Rougeard, and I needed to know why he'd been arrested again. The prospect of returning to the *hôtel de police* alone was not an attractive one, and I needed some moral support. Wendy was loitering in the kitchen, within earshot, making herself look busy.

'Wendy,' I said, 'where's Archie?'

'In the tractor hangar, I believe.'

'Okay, I'm taking him to Libourne. Should be back in time for lunch.'

I escaped through the front door before the old girl could buttonhole me about the phone call.

On the way into town I gave Archie an update on the case. He looked horrified when I revealed my audacious theft of The Badger's wine and the ridiculous wheelchair chase that followed. I told him that Hakim had been rearrested and that, as far as I was concerned, Lefèvre had got the wrong man. He seemed happy to accompany me and excited to be visiting the *hôtel de police*. Apparently, since Loubna's arrival, his interest in crime genre movies had become almost obsessive. I was far from sure that I approved, and when we arrived in Libourne, I'd learned rather more than I needed to know about Messrs Tarantino, Richie and Scorsese.

This time the squad room was all but empty. I reasoned that even policemen like to keep their Saturdays free. Pierre, however, was in his office. I could see him through the glazed door filling out some paperwork. He was wearing reading glasses and, I noticed, a pair of latex gloves. Beside a pile of forms on the desk sat a large clear evidence bag containing what looked like a wine-stained tablecloth. The guard who had accompanied us from the front desk tapped on the window and opened the door for us to enter.

'*Bonjour,* Jeanne,' Pierre said, half standing.

'*Bonjour,* Pierre, please don't get up. You remember Archie?'

The boy and Lefèvre said hello.

'Jeanne, there was no need for you to—'

I interrupted him. 'Why on earth have you arrested Hakim Watter again?'

Pierre removed his glasses, which had slid to the end of his nose, and polished them with a paper tissue, staring at me fixedly. He pointed to the evidence bag.

'That's why,' he said. 'Discovered this morning in a rubbish bin in the courtyard behind Wattar's apartment block.'

Pierre opened the bag and carefully lifted a corner of the white cloth. I looked again at the fabric; the scarlet stains were interspersed with patches of a much darker hue.

'A set of white overalls covered in what appears to be a mixture of red wine and blood.'

Strange, I thought, that the overalls weren't found during the initial search.

'Why now, Pierre? How come your men have only just found them?'

'Jeanne, according to you The Badger's supplier was a North African. I was obliged to tell the chief what you'd said, and he insisted on another, more thorough search of the premises. It doesn't look good for Wattar.'

I couldn't believe it. I was sure that the man Lefèvre

should be looking for was big – and hairy; Hakim was slight and balding. Plus, Hakim had said that his attacker was wearing white . . .

'Look, there's something else I should tell you. After my morning with The Badger, I went to the bar in Les Eglisottes—'

'I know. You met with John Clare in the Bar des Sports.'

'What!' I said incredulously. 'How the hell do you know that?'

'Jeanne, you are an Englishwoman who drives a tangerine-coloured *deux cheveaux* – you are . . . conspicuous.'

'Well, okay! And, yes, I did see John and I also talked to *le patron* – he said that a big, bearded North African was in the bar on the day that Rougeard and Hakim were arrested. Sounds like the same man who sold the wine to The Badger, eh? Big and hairy – Hakim is neither! And the overalls match his description of the intruder, right?'

Pierre considered my theory, pressed the air out of the bag and resealed it.

'I am aware of the bar owner's testimony. The man seen in the bar is not necessarily the same one who sold the wine. The Badger uses a wheelchair, Jeanne. Perhaps everyone looks big from that perspective. As for the beard, I don't know, maybe Wattar forgot to shave. And as of the white robed intruder, what did he call it – a jinn? It could be psychological . . . an alter ego . . . anything.'

I didn't buy it. Lefèvre was clearly desperate to charge somebody, anybody, to placate his boss. I wondered how a woman in a bar could be reported to the police immediately, but the brutal murder of a winemaker and a pair of blood-and-wine-soaked overalls could go undiscovered for several days.

'What about the wine, Pierre? Did you get the analysis done?'

'The laboratory confirmed that your wine is Château Cheval Blanc 1990, but there were no prints, nothing to prove it was from the same batch found at Wattar's place.'

Standing beside me, Archie began to fidget.

'Well,' I said, 'I suppose we should be going. I still don't think—'

'Sulphur.' Archie muttered.

'I'm sorry Archie, what did you say?'

'I think the overalls have sulphur on them.'

Pierre held up the bag. 'Well, *jeune homme*, we haven't had them analysed yet, but it looks like wine and blood to me.'

Again, Archie spoke. 'It's merlot, recent vintage; blood, I don't know what sort; and hydrogen sulphide in small quantities. I smelled it when you squeezed the air out.'

Pierre re-opened the bag, sniffed, then beckoned the boy to him. 'Smell it again.'

Archie moved closer to the bag, closed his eyes and inhaled gently. 'Yep,' he said. 'Sulphur.'

I'd parked near Place Decazes, so we walked back to the car through Libourne's narrow cobbled streets. Tuning into the Rue Gambetta I spotted the thermometer above the pharmacy door; it read thirty-one degrees. The forecast for the days to come was warm and dry. Tomorrow we would begin the merlot harvest, followed by the cabernets in the middle of the week. This would be one of my earliest harvests, but the fruit was more than ready. I bought an armful of baguettes from the bakery to feed my team: tonight the grape pickers would arrive anticipating the traditional welcome feast. They would occupy the little gîtes that flank the winery, eat, drink and be merry, and make far too much noise. Now all investigative (and romantic) thoughts were on hold until my vines were bare. We drove back to Fontloube with the roof down and my spirits up – for the time being.

Dimanche 11 Séptembre 2011

Turk's barking woke me at seven o'clock. It's the same every year; it always takes him a couple of days to get used to our visitors – the Spaniards, North Africans and Eastern Europeans who make up my motley brigade of grape pickers. Sunrise was due at seven-twenty, but the sky was bright already. From my bedroom window I could see the topmost vine leaves glowing in the dawn, barely stirred by the lightest of breezes. It would be a perfect day for the work ahead of us.

Archie would attack the lower slopes using the *enjambeur* – the skinny vineyard tractor – and, over the next few days, bring in a good half of the crop. The tractor is quick but indiscriminate; for the old vines I prefer to use old methods. I would rally my foot soldiers on the higher ground, where the grapes are picked by hand, leaving Loubna at the winery to operate the Mistral – the magic machine that strips away the stalks, chucks out the immature and rotten fruits and fills the vats with beautiful, perfect grapes.

We started at seven-thirty. I donned a straw hat, hoisted a grape hod onto my shoulders, picked up an empty plastic crate and joined my team on the côte. Once we'd got into the swing of it, the work progressed smoothly, and by lunchtime we'd harvested a third of a hectare. The fruit was perfect. Exhausted by the morning's work, we ambled back to the hangar to rest in the shade and eat our lunch of bread, cheese and duck rillettes, washed down with litres of water and a little *pinard* – the rough red wine reserved for my pickers. Several of the workers dozed beneath the horse chestnuts, and others sat cross-legged on the grass, smoking roll-ups and chatting. I took a stroll through the lower vines, checking the trellises, making sure the tractor had done its job, and recalling the events of the season. This year's fruit had escaped frost and hail, taken the early springtime in its stride, survived July's deluge, resisted forty-degree days in June and August, and dodged the thunder storms of September. It always strikes me as a minor miracle that we have any fruit at all. My mind then turned to previous harvests, making comparisons, recalling the temperatures and rainfall, the sugar levels and yields of past vintages. I spotted Archie driving down the côte on the tractor, a battered Panama shading his young face. God, he looked like his dad. Memories of that other harvest, three years ago, suddenly derailed my train of thought.

In 2008, it was Archie's father, Andrew, who had helped me with the harvest. That was during the early days of his illness, only months before he died. For a businessman and amateur poet he'd proved himself a capable winemaker. Since his passing, my memories were sustained by Archie's presence, and I'd often mistaken the boy for his father's ghost. Andrew was still with me, in many ways, making me laugh with corny one-liners, piercing my heart with his poetry.

Tears pricked my eyes. I leant back against a trellis stake, took out my handkerchief, and blew my nose. A long-forgotten remark of Andrew's concerning Captain Lefèvre came back to me. One morning, towards the end of Andrew's treatment, we'd received a visit from the policeman. Later, Andrew had said something like: 'You'll be alright with him, Jeanne, after I'm gone'. Of course, I was scandalized, and probably told him not to be so stupid. But here I was, bringing in another harvest, falling in love with Pierre Lefèvre and weeping for the man who'd picked him out for me. Thankfully, before I'd begun to consider

Pierre's feelings for me (or rather the lack thereof) Archie arrived to tell me I was needed in the winery.

After a perfect morning, the afternoon proved troublesome. The de-stemming machine gave up de-stemming, the conveyor belt refused to convey; and, having drunk too much wine at lunch, one of my best workers stopped working. By the end of the day we'd fixed most of the problems, but harvested only half a hectare of vines. Still, the juice was flowing and the weather forecast was good, so from now on everything would go smoothly.

Or so I hoped.

Lundi 12 Séptembre 2011

I woke at five a.m., tried to get back to sleep and failed.

I'd been dreaming about John Clare, and in the dream he had an identical twin. The pair were in a Fleet Street newsroom, typing on old-fashioned typewriters, desperate to make a copy deadline. They had to write a report about a murder, but although each twin insisted that his version was correct, the stories conflicted. The typewriter keyboards had black-and-white piano keys instead of letters. Each twin played a different tune; neither could play in harmony with the other.

Now, fully awake, with dawn's glimmer behind the curtains, two conflicting scenarios occupied my mind.

In one, I could see a big North African man, watching René Rougeard in the Bar des Sports, plotting a burglary and a murder. He waited until the following day, when Rougeard had been released from the *gendarmerie*, went to Lacasse dressed in white overalls, murdered his victim, and stole his computer and a few cases of very expensive wine. He then broke into Hakim Wattar's flat wearing a hood to hide his face, frightened him out of his wits, and left him with a liquid temptation he knew the young man could not resist. Later, he returned to the flat, threatened Hakim at knifepoint, and told him to accept God's judgement. Before leaving, he removed his bloody overalls and dumped them in Hakim's wheelie bin. What was left of the wine he sold to The Badger.

In this scenario, assuming it was a burglary, why

would the thief wait for Rougeard to be released? Surely it would have been simpler to break into Château Lacasse with its owner locked up in a police cell. If, however, it was a vengeance killing, why try to frame Hakim?

So, it wasn't just a burglary; nor was it just a psychopathic attack – could it have been both?

In the second scenario, I could see Hakim Wattar, exploited by his ex-employer and slighted by his insults, shamed by the fight in the bar, and short of money. I could imagine him stealing some valuable wine and computer equipment to pay the debt which was owed to him. I could see a confrontation with Rougeard, a fracas perhaps, even a violent one. I tried to see Hakim forcing Rougeard to climb the winery steps, slitting his throat and dumping his lifeless body into the vat.

But why would Hakim remove the contents of Rougeard's filing cabinet? What did he do with the files and the computer? Why make up the story about the jinn? In this scenario, Hakim Wattar must have had some very strange motives and a very peculiar psychology.

Perhaps Hakim and the big man were in cahoots. Perhaps they were jihadists. Or perhaps the jinn really did exist. Perhaps I was going crazy.

One thing alone was clear to me: the computer and the files would, I was sure, reveal all.

Another question bothered me: why the hell did I think Victor Lemaitre was involved? Well, Rougeard drove a vehicle purchased from Lemaitre's Mercedes dealership. He'd made a small fortune gambling in Lemaitre's casino. As well as cars and croupiers, Lemaitre owned a large wine export company. But as well as these facts, I just had a bad feeling about the man. Perhaps I should talk it over with Pierre.

At lunchtime I made the call. His mobile rang only once before he picked up.

'*Bonjour*, Jeanne.'

He sounded awful.

'*Bonjour*, Pierre. How's it going?'

'Not well. I'm off the case.'

'What the—? Why's that?'

'The chief wants a charge against Wattar, or at least to keep him in custody until after the weekend. He's put Folliot on the case, and I'm on admin duties.'

So, that explained his gloomy mood. 'Oh, God. It just doesn't make sense! I've been up since five o'clock thinking about it. Hakim couldn't have done it!'

'No? Listen, Jeanne, Hakim Wattar knew the victim, and the property. He lives nearby. He had two motives: the money owed to him, and the fight in the bar. Plus you said that The Badger received the wine from a North African. I think a jury might not agree with you.'

'Pierre, I'm sure Victor Lemaitre knows something.'

A second's silence. 'Jeanne, be very careful about making accusations against Monsieur Lemaitre. Until now I have not discouraged you; but, *please*, if you want to help me now just finish your harvest and leave this case alone.'

After the conversation I lingered in the study, staring out at the vines, wondering as I always do if this year they would make any money.

Château Fontloube's vineyards cover four hectares, about half of which are planted on the south-western slopes of the limestone côte. For each hectare, the rules allow me to produce up to five thousand litres of Saint-Emilion wine. Of course, I don't make anywhere near that. Most years we get about three-to-four thousand litres per hectare – quality rather than quantity, you see. That means that each year I make about twelve thousand litres of wine. Sixteen thousand bottles. Around thirteen hundred cases. A lot of wine for me to sell.

I'm lucky because most of my wine is sold to individuals or to local restaurants. A wine merchant in Saint James's, London also buys a good amount, some of which ends up at a very regal address in Windsor . . . So,

I'm fortunate to be able to sell what I make, but Fontloube is not a big business. At the end of the year, if I can settle the bills, keep my creditors happy and pay my itinerant workers, I have just enough left to survive on. Not that I'm complaining; I have everything I need – well, nearly.

It's much harder for winemakers like John Clare. He produces red Bordeaux – a wine worth far less than Saint-Emilion. He has only two hectares, so selling his produce direct to a broker might make John about ten thousand euros a year. Selling a few bottles at the cellar door brings in some extra income, but winemaking was more of a hobby than a livelihood for John.

René Rougeard had faced the same dilemma, although he did have more vines. How big was the property? John had said twelve hectares. Twelve hectares of Bordeaux *ordinaire* might produce a turnover of, say, sixty thousand euros before costs and tax – hardly a king's ransom, and surely not enough to pay for all the high-tech equipment at Château Lacasse, not to mention a shiny new Mercedes. So, unless he'd won it at the casino, how had Rougeard come into his small fortune?

I decided to ignore Pierre's advice and do a little digging. I couldn't turn my back on the harvest, but I could redeploy my resources. It was time to see if Loubna's talents extended to market research and corporate investigation.

By Monday evening we'd harvested one-and-a-half hectares of merlot vines, and around six thousand litres of grapey mush was macerating in my vats. Loubna and I were in the study, noting the day's figures, each massaging our aching shoulders, arms and legs.

'How are you finding the harvest, Loubna?' I asked.

She flashed me a green-eyed smile. 'Oh, it is very good, thank you. The work is not too hard, and it is much hotter in Morocco.'

'Well, I'm just going to make a phone call, and if all goes well, you can work here in the office tomorrow.

Would that be okay?'

'Okay, as you like, Jeanne. But who will take my place outside?'

'Hi, John. It's Jeanne.'

'Oh, hello, Jeanne. I was just going to call you to see how everything's going.'

'Everything's fine, John. The team are on form – with one or two exceptions – but they're all set to finish here on Thursday and start with you on Friday.'

'Great! I can't wait to see them.'

'Any news about Hakim?'

A deep sigh. 'No, they won't tell me anything and even the lawyer is getting nowhere.'

'Look, John, I have a couple of theories I want to test. I'm going to ask Loubna to help me look into Rougeard's business dealings. I can't promise it'll come to anything, but I've got to try.'

'Okay . . . ?'

'Problem is, I'll be a pair of hands short tomorrow. Would you—?'

'Jeanne, you can count me in. I'll be there – what time?'

'Great! Seven alright?'

'No problem. Can I bring the dogs?'

'Sure, but what about Turk?'

'Oh, they're not aggressive. They wouldn't harm a Jack Russell.'

'It's not Turk I'm worried about,' I said, laughing. 'He has a nasty bite, you know.'

'I'll tell Dorothy and Priscilla to be wary of him!'

'Okay,' I said, '*à demain.*'

'*A demain!*'

'Oh, by the way, do you sell any wine in bulk?'

'Afraid so, I'm trying to sell direct, but since I've been on my own – well, you know how difficult it is.'

I did, indeed. 'Who's your buyer?'

'La Girondine, in Libourne.'

'How long have you been working with them?'

'Since we arrived – when we bought the vineyards from Rougeard we carried on using the same *négoce*.'

'So, Rougeard was also selling to La Girondine?'

'I guess so.'

We said goodbye. My pulse quickened. So, I thought, that makes three things that link René Rougeard to Victor Lemaitre.

Mardi 13 Séptembre 2011

On Tuesday morning, once John had taken Loubna's place at the Mistral machine, she and I escaped to the cool of the study to begin our covert investigations.

I told her my thoughts about the case – that the stolen computer and the files might lead us to Rougeard's killer; that the posh wine, intended to frame Hakim, might have an ulterior significance; and that, aside from Lemaitre's dealings with Rougeard, I was highly suspicious of our future mayor. Perhaps I was expecting too much, but Loubna's brief was to find out all she could about Lemaitre's businesses, especially anything that involved Château Lacasse.

When I returned to the house at midday Wendy was sitting at the kitchen table, a glass of *pinard* in one hand and a copy of the *Guardian*, folded at the crossword, in the other. She peered at me over the rims of her reading glasses, stopped sucking the end of a biro.

'Musical instrument is in Bordeaux wine, eight letters?'

'Have you seen Loubna, Wendy?'

'Hmm? She's still in the study, my dear. I made her a sandwich.'

'Lucky her.'

'Solve the clue and I'll make you one too.'

'Oh, I'm useless at crosswords. Recorder?'

'No, my gorgeous, think about the wine. Go on, you can do it – the solution's in the clue . . .'

I got it: 'Clarinet?'

Wendy beamed. 'Bravo, Jeanne. Go through and I'll bring you something to eat.'

I found Loubna in the study, staring at the computer screen, fingers clicking at the keyboard.

'Okay, Loubna, how are you getting on?'

'Er . . .' she mumbled, finishing a line of text. 'Good, good. Have a look at these printouts.'

She hit the return key, then passed me a clear plastic folder containing several sheets of A4. I sat down opposite her, pulled out the papers and started to read the topmost page.

'That's a summary of Lemaitre's registered companies,' she said, resuming the clicking.

Some of the names I recognised; others on the list were unfamiliar to me.

'They're mostly holding companies, property businesses etcetera. The trading companies include S.A.R.L. Lemaitre Autos, Société Casino de Bordeaux and S.A.S. La Girondine – oh, and a chemical factory in Bassens, just outside the city.' She leaned across the desk and pointed to a name on the list: Soufrevin et Cie.

I read it out loud: 'Soufrevin and Company.'

'They make sulphur products for winemaking – pellets, powders, sticks . . .'

I remembered seeing their logo on the flammable sulphur sticks we use to sterilise our oak barrels. I also recalled the previous week's nightmare, the memory of which had all but faded leaving only the image of a white-feathered ghoul and the rotten-egg smell of sulphur . . .

'My God, Loubna—'

'What, Jeanne?'

'Sulphur! Sulphur's what Archie smelled on the clothing—'

Just then Wendy bustled in and presented me with lunch: a two-foot long baguette sandwich filled with what looked like an entire – and very ripe – camembert.

I stared at the enormous torpedo before me. 'Thanks Wendy,' I said. 'Still counting my calories, eh?'

'Eat, gorgeous girl. You need to keep your strength up. Now, what's all this about sulphur?'

I told her about Archie's olfactory analysis of the overalls, and this new discovery: that Victor Lemaitre owned a sulphur factory in Bordeaux. She stared at me blankly.

'Don't you see?' I said. 'Archie could smell sulphur on the clothes. Hakim said the white-robed intruder smelled of death. The murder victim drove a car bought from Lemaitre, gambled in Lemaitre's casino and sold his wine to a Lemaitre-owned company. And now, thanks to Loubna, we know that Lemaitre owns a company making sulphur products.'

Wendy scratched the back of her head. 'So, Lemaitre is the killer?'

'No! Well, I don't think so, Wendy – he doesn't seem like the murdering type to me. It's just a clue, that's all, like your eight-letter instrument. What did you say – the solution's in the clue? We've just got to solve it.'

She looked genuinely concerned. 'Oh, Jeanne, I think you should let Captain Lefèvre deal with clues and investigations and all that clever stuff. You shouldn't put yourself at risk, you know.'

First John, then Pierre, now Wendy. Even Loubna was nodding in agreement. Why was everybody so worried about me? 'Listen, both of you, Pierre's been taken off the case. His boss wants to charge Hakim for a crime he surely didn't commit. I don't trust Pierre's colleagues and I've promised John that I'll try to get Hakim out of jail. This sulphur factory could be the key to finding the real killer, and I think we should go and have a look around, okay?'

Wendy looked at Loubna; Loubna looked at me. 'Okay, Jeanne,' she said, 'as long as Wendy and I go with you.'

I gave it some thought – about a second's worth.

'Okay, ladies, tomorrow morning Archie and John can make a start on the cabernets, and we'll pop over to Bassens to sniff out this sulphur factory. Now, what's next?'

'Something else that smells a little . . . strange,' Loubna replied.

She wasn't referring to the camembert.

My young Moroccan intern, it seemed, was also a budding corporate investigator. Not only had she revealed Lemaitre's business interests, but she'd also discovered something rather puzzling about Rougeard's. The contents of the folder included three documents: the annual accounts for Château Lacasse from 2007 to 2009; a copy of the land registry *cadastre* showing the surface area of each of Rougeard's vineyards; and the *Arrêtée Portant Fixation du Prix (Dec 2009)* – an official government report which shows the market price of bulk-sold wines. The puzzle these documents presented was this: Rougeard sold all his wine to La Girondine, but the price he was being paid each year was increasing – much faster than inflation, and for way more than the market price. In 2007, his Bordeaux rouge was sold at 720€ per tonneau; in 2008 it was 930€; and by 2009 Rougeard was paid 1,170€ for the same wine. True, 2009 was an excellent vintage, but even so, the average price that year was only 840€ per tonneau. But even at these prices, the profits declared in the accounts were nowhere near enough for Rougeard to modernize his winery or buy a brand-new Mercedes.

After lunch, I left Loubna and Wendy in the study and went to join the gang in the vines. I asked John how much he was paid for his wine by La Girondine; apparently he got more-or-less the market price. Loubna was right: something smelled decidedly fishy. We finished the merlot harvest at seven p.m., and worked until ten in the winery. John was happy to cover for me the following morning, and he and Archie seemed to get on fine. I was beginning to understand that John was far more than a hobbyist, and now that the merlot crop had been put into the vats, I was less anxious about absenting myself for an hour or two. What harm could possibly come to us by going to Bordeaux to look at a factory? I'd call Pierre in the morning to tell him our plan, give him the address of the factory and charge my mobile phone. What could go wrong?

Mercredi 14 Séptembre 2011

Another hot night, another odd dream. I was on stage at the opera, lying naked in a hospital bed. Projected onto the black backdrop was Château Lacasse, illuminated like a giant Halloween mask, starring at me with malevolent eyes and a broken-toothed, leering grin. I knew that the house was the devil come to get me. I knew what I had to confess. I had killed my child, and now I was going to Hell. But in that peculiar way that things do in a dream, the devil house morphed into Pierre Lefèvre's face, the leer melted into a warm smile. 'It's not true, Jeanne,' the face said, 'this is just a fiction.' I closed my eyes, and when I opened them Pierre was sitting beside me on the bed. His warm hand caressed my fevered brow, my neck and bare chest, then slid under the bedcovers as he bent to kiss my trembling lips . . .

The alarm clock buzzed, and I was dragged into the morning's bright reality, happy to escape eternal damnation, but reluctant to leave the dream's erotic potential. In the shower, I thought about the corpse in the cuve and Rougeard's own cursed soul. I wondered what crime he could have committed to deserve such a punishment. Yes, he was a victim, but what possible provocation could have resulted in such a grisly, violent end? If the bearded man in the bar was the killer, could Rougeard's profane words alone have released such rage, such violence? Perhaps the murderer was a random serial killer with a grudge against winemakers; it didn't seem likely. A more likely explanation related, I suspected, to Rougeard's over-valued wine. The love of money is the root of all evil, as Paul put it. Was the corpse in the cuve a victim of his own avarice? Was Rougeard blackmailing Lemaitre, and if so, what was Lemaitre trying to hide? Motives aside, the factory in Bassens might at least explain why the killer's clothing smelled of sulphur.

A typical harvest breakfast – quick and simple – preceded John's arrival, but by the time I'd given him and Archie their instructions and made a call to Pierre it was past ten o'clock. Once John knew what he was doing and Pierre knew where we were going, I rounded up Wendy, Loubna and Turk, peeled back Clémentine's canvas roof and set off for Bordeaux. We took the scenic route via the bridge at Branne and through the vineyards of the Entre-deux-Mers. With the wind in our hair, a Fats Waller song playing on the radio, an old friend beside me and a new one in the back with my faithful dog, I was happy. Wendy kept us entertained with some tall tales of Sicily in the late '60s. Apparently, she and a young man had been arrested in Messina owing to a case of mistaken identity.

'. . . of course, my dears, the weapons were found the following day in the boot of a Lancia Flaminia, and the carabinieri had to let us go. Still, everyone was frightfully apologetic and I must say the meals they gave us were delicious.'

'What were they?' asked Loubna, from the back seat.

'What dear? Oh, I can't remember. Pasta dishes, mainly.'

I could hear Loubna giggling behind me. 'No, Wendy, I mean what kind of rifles were they?'

'Rifles? Ah, yes, I see. D'you know I can't remember that either. Big, long things – just why they thought we'd stolen them I still don't understand.'

'Probably Garands, 30-calibre,' Loubna said.

'Goodness, my dear, did you learn that from one of your gangster movies?'

'No, my grandfather has one. We go hunting together in the mountains – mostly rabbit, some pheasant, sometimes a Barbary boar.'

Well, you certainly can misjudge someone. 'You surprise me,' I said, eyeing Loubna in the rear-view mirror.

Wendy twisted round in the seat, the better to talk to her. 'Well, I'm not surprised, my gorgeous. You are a veritable Artemis, the archer goddess, protector of hunters; goddess, too, of the moon, the wilderness, virginity and childbirth . . . a young woman with remarkable powers.'

Loubna's reflection blushed. 'Oh, I don't think there's anything remarkable about me, Wendy,' she said, smiling to herself.

'That, my dear, remains to be seen. But I suspect that one day you will surprise everyone – including yourself.' She settled back in her seat and tapped the Saint Christopher that covers the bullet hole in Clémentine's dashboard. 'Just like Jeanne here. Did she ever tell you about this, my dear?'

I'd been reluctant to disclose last year's events to Loubna. A young intern, thousands of miles from home; she didn't need to know the gory details. Wendy had agreed to keep mum about it, too. But Wendy had never been a keeper of secrets.

I gave her the eye. 'Oh, I'm sure Loubna doesn't want to hear about all that.'

Wendy gazed out of the passenger-side window, adjusting her dentures noisily. Loubna leaned forward, gripping the rail on the back of the seat. 'Well,' she said, 'I am curious. What did you do, Jeanne?'

Oh, well, I thought, here goes.

'Last year Captain Lefèvre's brigade was trying to catch a gang of international drug traffickers. The narcotics police – *les stups*, I think they say – had set a trap for the gang at Bordeaux airport. But their informers had misled them; the drugs were arriving by sea. The organisation was transporting hundreds kilos of cocaine by ship, hidden under a shipment of Albanian timber. After unloading the official cargo, they brought the drugs ashore in a little boat. I stumbled upon the gang as they were unloading the drugs at a fishing shack under the Aquitaine bridge. I was kidnapped by them, but Turk helped me escape. One of the men opened fire as I was driving away. I crashed the car, and a bullet grazed my neck and ended up in the dashboard. This Saint Christopher covers the hole and brings me luck, hopefully.'

'Cool,' Loubna said, reaching over to touch the lucky charm. 'Did the captain rescue you?'

'Luckily, Pierre was attending an armed robbery just the other side of the bridge, so he was the first on the scene. He sort of saved my life.'

'Then your destinies are surely linked, Jeanne. You owe him your life, and you may have to repay him one day.'

'I'm sure you'll think of something, Jeanne,' said Wendy.

It was my turn to blush.

Okay, I left out the bit about Aimée Loroux's murder; some things are better left unsaid.

The eleven o'clock news had just started when we reached the outskirts of the city. We drove through Lormont, not far from the Aquitaine bridge, and arrived in Bassens – an unremarkable area of low-rise industrial units, ugly factories and riverside derricks. Our destination on Rue Manon Cormier was easy to find. The huge factory complex seemed to be deserted as we drove past its crumbling concrete units and rusty steel structures. Clearly this square kilometre of post-industrial decay had once been an impressive enterprise, but now it looked like a ghost town. It felt as though our journey had been a waste of time, and I was about to suggest lunch in the city when Loubna spotted a security guard sitting in a small brick-and-glass kiosk. I parked a little way from the guard and waved to him. He came out of his hut and strolled towards us. Mistaking us for a trio of lost tourists, he looked quite surprised when I told him we were looking for Soufrevin's HQ. Nor did his confused expression alter when I explained that I was a winemaker. We were told, rather brusquely, that the company did not trade from these premises and that I should enquire at their retail outlet, a few kilometres upriver in Floirac. I asked, casually, if the products were made here in Bassens. Apparently the manufacturing process had moved to the Far East, but a small team remained, transforming and packaging the sulphur products.

Bingo, I said to myself.

We drove a couple of blocks, parked up in the shade between two giant silos and waited. At midday Soufrevin's workers would surely down tools for lunch, return home or go to a local bistro. Sure enough, at noon we heard the sound of doors shutting and watched a few cars rumble past us. None of the vehicles' occupants fitted the descriptions of the suspect, and again I considered giving up and following the traffic to the nearest eatery. I was about start the motor when another vehicle approached, this time a white van. In the time it took for the van to pass our hideaway I got a good look at the driver: a well-built, bearded man – possibly North African or Midde-Eastern – wearing a white tunic.

That's our man, I thought. Now, let's see where he lives – or at least where he eats.

I waited a few seconds before pulling out, then followed the van out of the factory compound, turning right onto the main road in the direction of town. Keeping a hundred metres or so between us and the van, we motored under the railway lines and into a busy commercial district. Here we met the lunch-hour traffic and joined a line of slow-moving vehicles driven, no doubt, by hungry French workers en route to their midday meal. After the third or fourth roundabout, several cars had come between us, and, at the next junction, we lost him. It seemed that all of Bordeaux's white vans were out and about today, but I drove on regardless, desperately trying to recognise our man. Red traffic lights had caused a jam up ahead. There, near the front of the queue was a white van, its left indicator flashing; it looked like the right vehicle. I waited impatiently for the lights to change, revved Clémentine's engine and crawled towards the junction. The van turned left into a residential street, and by the time we reached the lights they had changed to amber. The car in front jumped the light, and I followed suit, dropped a gear and sped through the intersection to a chorus of klaxons. Our man, a couple of hundred metres ahead, slowed and took another left in the direction of the river. Keeping a safe distance, we followed the van out of the town and into the port district on the Garonne's right bank. Here there were no restaurants, no bars, no apartment blocks, just container parks, spindly crane derricks and the bridge's huge profile looming ahead of us. I'd never tailed anyone before, and I had a bad feeling that my first attempt might not be going to plan. The van was the only vehicle ahead of us; in the rear view mirror the road was empty. I began to feel a tad exposed, and decided to call it a day. I pulled up on the dockside and cut the motor. Apart from a sickly-looking seagull perched on a fence between us and the river, we were the only souls to witness the van disappear into the distance.

Not for the first time I wondered what the hell I was doing. 'Okay, *mesdames*,' I sighed. 'Time to call it a day. Perhaps we should let the police deal with all this.'

'Lunchtime?' Wendy said.

'Chez Stéphane?' I said.

'Oh, goody!' Wendy said. 'Such hungry work being a private eye.'

We followed the port road towards the bridge, passing container ships and other smaller vessels moored up on the dock. To our left were hundreds of shipping containers; to our right, the broad river's shimmering waters. The road took a sharp left turn and, without prior warning, brought us to metal barrier bearing a yellow sign that read: ROUTE BAREE.

'Typical,' I said, throwing the stick-shift into reverse. 'We'll just have to go back the way we came.'

I made a three-point turn and drove back towards the river, swung round the bend and there, coming towards us at speed, was the white van. I stood on the brakes and we skidded to a halt, bumper to bumper, inches away from the van's radiator. I stared at the grille badge – a three-pointed star. Each of us looked up, slowly. At the wheel was the bearded man, glaring at us.

'Oh, shit,' I whispered.

Wendy's hand found mine. 'Don't worry, dear, I'm sure he'll let us pass.'

Loubna was silent. Turk growled menacingly.

The bearded face stared down at us through Clémentine's open roof. A pair of dark, menacing eyes blinked once then closed; lips – pink and sensitive amid a crow's nest of beard – began to mouth the words of some inaudible incantation. Was he praying? Uttering a curse? He opened his eyes and focused his attention on us once more. The van's door opened an inch. I took the phone from the glove box, desperately hoping that Wendy was right, but fearing the worst: we were all going to die.

In the time it took for me to bring up Pierre's number, the man had stopped staring and was now lowering the driver's side window to adjust the wing mirror. He seemed distracted by something in the mirror, unseen by us, behind the van.

Without warning he reversed at speed and, after a deft handbrake turn, drove off towards the town.

A river police boat – surely the cause of the bearded man's hasty departure – drew alongside the quay. Two uniformed officers and a customs guard disembarked and waved farewell to their colleagues onboard.

'I think we should go home,' I said.

'Yes, dear, I think you're right.'

Just then the phone rang. It was Pierre.

'You called me, Jeanne?'

'Oh, yes,' I said, flustered. 'I must have pressed a button by mistake.'

'Are you okay?'

'Of course. We're fine – aren't we ladies?'

Wendy and Lubna both said yes.

'Where are you?'

'Still in Bordeaux. We went to have a look at the factory, like I said.'

'Did you see anything interesting, suspicious, unusual?'

'Well . . . we have just seen a big bearded man wearing a white tunic.'

'Jeanne, I want you to drive to Libourne and meet me outside the *hôtel de police*, okay?'

'But, we haven't had lunch yet—'

'Never mind. Just come, please.'

Lunch hour in Libourne, and nowhere to park near the police station. We trawled the town's labyrinth of one-way streets – all mercifully free of white commercial vehicles – and eventually found a space on Rue Clément Thomas. To be back on home turf, after the stressful encounter with the bearded man, was a welcome solace. Tantalizing aromas wafted from every bakery, brasserie and restaurant as we walked to the station. I noticed Wendy scanning menu boards with a wistful eye. We were all hungry.

A few metres away from the station's main doors stood Pierre, chatting with a portly guard. A roll-up cigarette, which had adhered itself the guard's lower lip, danced up and down as he talked. I recognised him as one of the officers who'd helped empty the vat in Rougeard's winery. As we approached, the two men shook hands and said '*à tout à l'heure*'. The officer disappeared inside the station and Pierre came over to greet us.

'*Bonjour, mesdames,*' he said, taking my arm and directing us to the public gardens on the opposite side of the street. 'Let us go and look at the beautiful flowers.'

We strolled into the park, admiring the late summer blooms and tidy lawns, and found a bench near the war memorial. My friends sat down, and Turk hopped onto Loubna's lap. Pierre and I continued towards the memorial's granite plinth on which sat a bronze statue, at once tragic and triumphant, that I had never noticed before: a wounded soldier in the arms of a young woman watched over by a winged angel holding two laurel crowns. We stopped and read the inscription: *Aux Morts Glorieux* – to our glorious dead.

'They both suffered, and yet they will both be saved,' Pierre said.

'What? Ah, yes, the man and the woman.'

'I think that is the message – or one of them.'

'Our sacrifices will be rewarded in heaven. Do you believe that, Pierre?'

'Jeanne, these days I am not sure what I believe. Now, tell me what you found in Bassens, and I will tell you something about Hakim Wattar's case.'

Should I relate the whole story, or omit the terrifying bit?

'Okay. We went to the factory. Not much goes on there now – but a security guard told us that a small team still processes and packs the sulphur products. We waited until lunchtime and then – you won't believe it – we saw him.'

Pierre looked unimpressed. 'Saw . . . who, exactly?'

'The bearded man! Well, a guy who looks just like the descriptions.'

'Descriptions?'

'Yes, Pierre, the *descriptions*. Hakim's – a man with evil eyes wearing a white tunic; the barman's – a big, bearded North-African; and the Badger's – a big, hairy Arab. We saw him, Pierre, driving a van large enough to transport several cases of stolen wine. We saw him and he saw us!'

'What do you mean – he saw you?'

I feared a telling-off might result if I told Pierre the

whole truth, so I gave him the censored version.

'We waited in the factory compound and the man drove past us in a white van. We got a good look at his face and clothing and he looked at us, you know, suspiciously. I'm sure he's our man, Pierre. I'm sure of it.'

Pierre folded his arms and then scratched his stubbly chin. 'Okay, it's a lead. But there's nothing I can do now to investigate it. Foliot is watching me.'

I like to think I'm a courageous person, but only Pierre or his colleagues had the wherewithal to catch the bearded man – I had no idea how to proceed and wouldn't want to repeat this morning's encounter. Surely there was something he could do.

'You're on admin duties, right?'

He nodded.

'So, run some checks on Soufrevin, see if they employ anyone like the man I saw.'

'If only it were that straightforward. You can't make enquiries like that without leaving a trail – the computer knows all and sees all.'

I stared at the tragedy in bronze above us. The scene recalled a distant, blurred memory I was reluctant to bring into focus. The morning's joy had been replaced, yet again, by melancholy.

'So, what about Hakim?' I asked.

'Ah, yes. Jonzac just told me that Commandant Foliot is running out of reasons to detain him. The forensics team analysed hairs and fibres taken from the corpse – the fibres match the white overalls, but the hairs do not match Wattar's DNA.'

'Jonzac?'

'He's working on the case – you saw him just now.'

'Yes, I met him the night we went to Lacasse. You said he was a good man.'

'Did I? Well, yes, he is.'

'So . . . why don't you ask him to check the factory's payroll?'

Pierre, a little exasperated, glanced up at the angel

and sighed. 'Alright, he owes me a favour—'

'Good. Now, why else did you want to meet?'

He touched my arm with a warm hand, his expression kindly but stern.

'Jeanne, I wanted to tell you something. You are convinced, are you not, that Hakim Wattar is innocent? If that is true, then the person who did murder René Rougeard is out here somewhere. Your assistance in the case, from the beginning, has been invaluable. But now you must do something for me, Jeanne. You must stay away from anything or anyone connected with all this.'

Both his hands were holding my shoulders now. If it hadn't been for Wendy and Loubna, there on the bench chatting, I'd have cried like a child. If only Pierre would tell me how he felt about me – one simple expression of emotion – then I would gladly comply with anything he asked of me, and everything would be alright.

'Jeanne,' he said quietly, glancing over his shoulder at the others, 'you are very special to me – you know that don't you?'

I nodded. *Special* was one step up from *charming*, I suppose.

I don't want anything bad to happen to you, okay?'

'Okay,' I said.

'Now, I propose to take you to lunch.'

'Hear that, Loubna,' Wendy said, 'our prayers have been answered!'

She'd clearly been eavesdropping on the entire conversation.

We'd been the lunchtime shift's last customers at the little bistro on Rue Gambetta, and the service had been brisk. But, after eating *Landaise* salad, grilled trout *aux amandes*, cheese and dessert, it was nearly three o'clock when we left Libourne. Loubna fell asleep on the back seat with the dog, and Wendy, beside me, snored loudly all the way home.

Between them, Archie and John had filled a nine-hundred litre tank with cabernet franc grapes and had begun to fill another. They too had had a productive day. I told John to go home and rest, but he stayed, and by evening both tanks were full. Tomorrow we would finish the cabernet harvest and my grape pickers' work would be done – at least at Fontoube; they still had to start John's harvest on Friday. Tradition dictated, however, that tomorrow evening we would celebrate with an al fresco vineyard dinner, and this year I was hoping that Pierre would be there to celebrate with me.

Jeudi 15 Séptembre 2011

First thing Thursday morning, I asked Loubna to help me with something that had kept me awake half the night. This was the crux of it: Rougeard was selling over-priced wine to a company owned by Lemaitre; he drove a car bought from Lemaitre's Mercedes dealership; he gambled in Lemaitre's casino; and, if I was right, he was killed by one of Lemaitre's employees. It seemed that Rougeard had some sort of hold over Lemaitre – until, that is, he was murdered. My hunch was that Lemaitre was being blackmailed. We just needed to find out how. I asked my ace investigator to do some more digging into Lemaitre's business dealings and went out to join the others for the last day of the harvest.

By the end of the morning we'd finally stripped bare all the cabernets and the remaining merlots, de-stemmed and sorted the fruit and filled every available vat in the winery. This year was a bumper crop: fifteen thousand litres in all. In the afternoon the vineyard and winery equipment was cleaned and tidied, and I went into the house to take a shower before helping Wendy with preparations for the harvest supper.

I'd just come downstairs, my hair wrapped up in a towel turban, when Loubna rushed into the kitchen.

'Jeanne,' she said, clearly excited, 'I think you should come and see this.'

I followed her to the study and we sat down opposite each other at the desk. A little out of breath, she inhaled deeply before speaking. 'I think I have discovered something odd about La Girondine's business.'

'Go on,' I said.

'I spoke to someone there earlier – an intern, like me. He's studying for a Masters in Oenology at the University of Dijon. Dominic is his name. Anyway, I told him I was doing some research on the Bordeaux wine trade – geographic distributions, market sectors and so on. I asked if he could tell me La Girondine's main market sectors, and he agreed. The information was purely for academic research purposes, of course.'

'Of course,' I said.

'He told me that the USA is La Girondine's main export market, and that the majority of their production is sold to a multi-billion-dollar drinks company in Minneapolis called MidWest Brewers Inc.'

'Sounds like a good client,' I said.

'A very good client – they are in the top one hundred. Anyway, I waited till three o'clock to call MidWest—'

'You called them?'

'Sorry, Jeanne,' she said, turning bashful, 'I should have asked you before making the call—'

'Good Lord, no, Loubna. I'm just impressed you took the initiative.'

'Oh. I see.' Her excited smile returned. 'So, I called the company in Minneapolis and spoke to someone in the public relations department. It was only eight a.m. there and I think the person I spoke to was not very senior. Anyway, he sounded like a nice young man and I said I was researching the distribution of Bordeaux wines in North America—'

'For research purposes?'

'Yes, of course. He said they buy wine from several prestigious wine villages and sell it under a label called Thomas Jefferson's Cellar. He emailed me a list of the villages along with volumes bought. They buy all their Saint-Emilion wine from La Girondine – it's their best seller.'

I was struggling to keep pace with Loubna's account.

'Loubna, how did you get a major drinks company to send you their sales figures?'

'Well, not sales figures exactly, just the volumes. And, as I say, he was very helpful and kind. I think he was on an internship too – going back to college at the end of the month.'

I was starting to suspect that the world of commerce was run by student interns.

'Okay,' I said, 'but what's so interesting about that?'

'Here's the list,' she said, passing me a printout.

The sheet showed a list of Bordeaux *appellations*, each with a corresponding figure of the volume of wine sold.

'So?' I said.

'Look at the sales of Saint-Emilion.'

I scanned down the list and found the figure; it was a big number – so big I could hardly believe it.

'My God, Loubna, over ten million bottles. That can't be right, can it?'

'Not unless they are buying nearly all the region's production.'

'And they buy all their wine from La Girondine, you say?'

'Yes, that's what he told me.' she said.

I thought about it for a couple of seconds. That La Girondine was exporting nearly all the region's wine was impossible; the alternative was obvious.

'Then the stuff they're buying isn't Saint-Emilion!'

'I told you it was a bit odd.'

'And if Rougeard knew what Lemaitre's company was doing—'

'Then maybe it was blackmail?'

'Loubna,' I said, 'you are a genius.'

By late morning, preparations for the *méchoui* were well underway. This Moroccan feast, a legacy of France's colonial past, is a yearly fixture at Fontloube. The pickers were digging a fire pit over which a whole lamb would be roasted. The rickety iron spit on which the meat is skewered always looks like something from a medieval torture chamber, but the results are delicious. To go with the meat, Loubna had prepared a *couscous* – a huge pot of braised Mediterranean vegetables in a rich, spicy tomato sauce with a mountain of steamed semolina to soak up the juices. It's perfect for an alfresco party and there's something for everyone – pork abstainers and vegetarians included. In the afternoon the fire was lit, and soon the tantalizing aromas of smoky roast lamb, olive oil and pungent rosemary drifted into the study where I sat adding up the grape pickers' wages.

I called Pierre to tell him my hunch that La Girondine was selling counterfeit Saint-Emilion in to the Americans. He wanted to know if we had proof. Loubna's printouts, he said, might be enough to justify an investigation. He would come to collect the documents in the evening, and of course, I asked him to stay for dinner. Apparently, he was off duty but 'on call' – a distinction I didn't fully grasp – but if he could be with us for the *méchoui* I was happy.

As well as the grape pickers and the captain, the other guests would include John Clare, Wendy, Archie and Loubna, my restaurant friend Stéphane, his wife Isabelle, and their three charming children; over twenty of us in all.

By seven p.m. everyone, except Pierre, was seated at the trestle tables Archie had set out on the lawn. After the toasts and leg-pulling that always precede this annual feast, Wendy and Loubna brought out platters of Bayonne ham, artichoke hearts, Provencal olives and great slabs of *paté de campagne*. Dinner was in full swing when Pierre arrived, so I excused myself and took him to the study to look at Loubna's findings.

Dressed for a warm evening in cotton shirt and slacks, Pierre looked more like a holidaymaker than a captain of police. His manner, too, was more relaxed than usual. I was afraid he might dismiss our findings with professional contempt, but he examined Loubna's printouts with genuine enthusiasm.

'This is fascinating, Jeanne. So, the wine sold by Lemaitre to the American company, and then sold as Saint-Emilion, isn't Saint-Emilion?'

'Well, not all of it. It can't be. The region produces about sixteen million bottles of *grand cru* wine. According to the Americans, Lemaitre ships them two-thirds that amount every year. There's no way that one Bordeaux broker can be trading that much wine. Something is very, very wrong.'

'And Lemaitre bought all Rougeard's crop, yes?'

'Yes and paid him way over the odds.'

'Okay, leave it with me Jeanne.' He held up the printout. 'I look forward to seeing Lemaitre's reaction to this.'

'What will you do? I thought you were off the case.'

'Tomorrow, I think I may visit the Casino.'

When we joined the party Pierre shook hands with everyone, kissed the ladies and sat at the head of the table flanked by Wendy and Archie. He chatted amiably with both, and teased and joked with the Laverne children – an avuncular role which suited him well. The sun set behind the horse chestnuts and someone took out a battered old guitar. Before the main course was finished the singing and dancing began. The rotisserie was hauled away from the fire pit and dry vine cuttings thrown onto the embers. I watched as Wendy and John joined the others dancing round the bonfire. Loubna coaxed Archie, a reluctant dancer, to follow them, and Pierre came over to my end of the table and took my hand. For a police captain he was a good dancer and he didn't tread on my toes too much. At the end of the song he held me in his arms and gave me a kiss – brief, soft, and tender.

Temporarily exhausted, we came back to the table to continue the feast. More dancing followed the lamb and the couscous, and by the time we'd finished the enormous cheeseboard and the pyramid of profiteroles that Stéphane had provided it was nearly midnight. The children fell asleep on the grass with the dogs, the Milky Way gave us a wondrous lightshow, and soon everyone was either too full or too tipsy to dance. I said goodnight to Stéphane and Isabelle, and then helped Wendy back to the house. Loubna and Archie were quick to follow, and John thanked me again for a wonderful evening before taking his leave.

I took a half-empty bottle and two glasses and led Pierre away from the bonfire to relax on a couple of wooden deck chairs under the trees. He filled my glass, then his, and we toasted each other's health.

'Thank you, Jeanne,' he said, 'for a most enjoyable evening. I must say, the life of a winemaker is indeed a charmed one.'

'It's not all harvest celebrations and drinking, you know. This week was bloody hard work I'll have you know – fifteen thousand litres, Pierre! And next it's the fermentation, then the malolactic, then the *soutirage*, the pruning, bottling last year's vintage . . . plus I have to sell the stuff.'

'Okay, but look at this,' he made an open-armed gesture encompassing the moonlit vineyard, the glowing fire and the revellers enjoying the last of the evening's warmth. '*C'est magnifique!*'

I couldn't argue with him. I adore this moment after the hard work of the harvest and before the even harder work of winter. It was magnificent.

'Yes, Pierre, you're right – if not I wouldn't do it.'

We sat in silence for a moment listening to a pair of owls call to each other in the tall beeches on the ridge.

'And anyway, what about you, Police Captain Lefèvre? You must have some incredible experiences.'

'Incredible is the word. You would not believe what human beings are capable of. And neither would you want to know.'

He was right: I was happy to remain ignorant of the worse aspects of his work.

'But apart from that,' I said, 'it must be rewarding – helping people, I mean. And then there's the camaraderie, the practical jokes, the macabre humour of the squad room . . .'

'Sometimes, a sense of humour is useful, yes.'

'I bet you've had some funny encounters.'

He poured what remained of the wine into our glasses. 'What, you mean criminals doing stupid things?'

I noticed a mischievous smile creep onto his face.

'That sort of thing, yes.'

'I don't want to bore you.'

'Tell!' I said, 'I love stories.'

He took a sip of wine. 'Well, an honest citizen once handed in a mobile phone that had been found on Place Decazes. The memory card contained hundreds of text messages between the phone's owner and his clients, all relating to the sale of illegal drugs. The owner was clearly a successful local dealer, though not so successful at covering his tracks. So, we sent a text message to each of the clients saying that a special deal was available – the buyer just had come to a particular hotel in Libourne and ask the concierge for the dealer by name.'

'Wow, did they take the bait?'

'Quite a few showed up at the hotel and asked to speak to the dealer. We already knew who he was, of course, via the phone company. Most of them were carrying something illegal, and those who agreed to testify against the man were released without charge. The dealer was devastated when we arrested him – *mon dieu,* he must have felt so stupid!'

I couldn't help laughing, more at Pierre's mordant sense of humour than the dealer's self-inflicted misfortune, and before I could ask him if the man was pleased to get his phone back, he'd segued into another story:

'Then there was the night a thief broke into a farmer's wine cellar on the Pomerol road. The owner called us to say that the thief had drunk the wine he'd intended to steal and was, by that stage, quite inebriated. The drunken thief then barricaded himself in and threatened to broach all the barrels with a pickaxe – his demands were unclear, but the owner was reluctant to risk his precious stocks of wine. We arrived at the scene and spoke to the intruder through a small ventilation duct outside. He refused to come out, and it looked like we had a long night's work ahead.

'Now, I knew the farmer quite well. He was a keen hunter – he and his friends enjoyed a day's *furetage* – you know, hunting rabbits with those little furry things with sharp teeth . . .'

'Ferrets?' I suggested.

'Yes, ferrets – I could see the wooden cages stacked up in an outbuilding next to the farmhouse. Anyway, I spoke to the thief, told him he might need the pickaxe to defend himself with because the cellar was full of vineyard rats – big strong creatures, well nourished on grapes, but now, after the harvest, desperately hungry.

'He told me to go and boil my head, so we cut the electricity and waited for the glow from the man's cigarette lighter to fade. Next, I told one of the men to lock the cellar door from the outside and slip a couple of ferrets into the ventilation duct.

'It did not take very long. We listened carefully to the sniffing, shuffling and squeaking sounds coming from the cellar. After that we heard the man screaming – like a devil in the font! – then the crashing sound of the barricade being torn down. He begged to be let out for several minutes before we unlocked the door.'

'You horrible man!' I said.

'Nonsense! The ferrets came to no harm.'

We laughed, drained our glasses, then lay back in the recliners, gazing at the stars. One of the grape pickers threw a vine root on the bonfire sending a swirl of sparks up into the night sky. Our hands touched, his fingers slowly interlocking with mine.

'Pierre,' I said. 'We are holding hands.'

'Don't you like it?'

'Of course I like it. I'm just not sure why we are doing it.'

He turned onto his side to face me. I looked at his face illuminated by the fire: his kindly, rugged features, his stubbly chin, his gentle smile, the sparks that flickered in his dark eyes. I liked what I saw – all of it. But what did he see, I wondered, looking at me? Did he like what he saw? Something told me he did.

It's now or never, Lefèvre, I said to myself.

'Jeanne?'

'Pierre?'

'Would you like to show me your room?'

'I would, Pierre, if you promise not to behave yourself.'

'I promise,' he said.

We crept away from the fireside like a couple of bashful teenagers, guilty of a secret fantasy we had yet to act out. Having sneaked into the house via the side door, we padded carefully up the stairs past Wendy's room, past Archie's, then stopped on the landing before entering mine.

'Are you sure?' I whispered.

He opened the door, followed me inside, turned the key in the lock. Apparently he was sure. I pulled him to me, and our lips touched in a tentative kiss, a sensual prelude to the overture to come.

My heart was doing strange things, and I felt a weird tingling sensation in my chest – was I having palpitations? I realised that Pierre's phone was buzzing in his shirt pocket.

He took the call.

'Lefèvre . . . .*Oui, Jonzac, ça va*...Where? . . . Why can't Folliot go? . . . *Merde*. Okay, fifteen minutes.'

The phone went back in Pierre's pocket, and he gave me that puppy dog look.

'Jeanne. I'm sorry, really sorry.'

'What is it?' I asked, following him onto the landing

and back down the stairs.

'A domestic siege at a skunk house in Libourne – the occupants resisted arrest, and now the man is holding his girlfriend hostage at knifepoint.'

'Oh, God,' I said. 'Must you go?'

'Folliot is at his wife's summer house in Nice until tomorrow. I am the only senior officer available.'

'Will you come back later?'

'I will try.'

'I'll leave the door unlocked, then?'

At this he turned to me and frowned. 'No, Jeanne, listen to me – keep the doors and windows locked tonight, okay?'

'Don't Pierre, you're scaring me.'

'Look, there is something I have to tell you. Jonzac made a *controle* of the sulphur factory's payroll. There's an Algerian working there called Abdul Grouazel. He could be the man you saw yesterday. Apparently he has quite a criminal record.'

'Good God, do you think he's . . . dangerous?'

'I don't know, Jeanne. Just stay at home and lock up, okay?'

'Okay,' I said, feeling more than a little anxious. 'But call me, will you? I'll leave the phone by the bed.'

'I will,' he said.

We kissed, as parting lovers do. I listened to his promises to come back as soon as he could, then stood on the front steps to watch my nearly-lover depart.

'Come on Turk,' I said to the little dog lingering at my feet. 'Let's see if there's anyone left.'

We crossed the courtyard to the lawn. The bonfire was still alight, but the last of the late-night revellers had, it seemed, gone to bed. I sat on the grass next to the fire pit, stroking Turk's ears and staring into the embers. Perhaps Pierre was right: perhaps I did have a charmed life. The harvest was a success, the evening had been enjoyed by all, my adopted family were all here with me – even old Turk. The man whose love I sought, it seemed, sought mine too. And, after twenty-five years, my hard work in these vines was to be recognised by my peers – those pillars of Saint-Emilion society, the Jurade. Blessings counted, I had to admit that life could be a lot worse.

So why did I still feel so empty? Was it because somewhere within the convoluted layers of my psyche lurked the thought that Pierre had come here tonight not to love me, but to protect me?

I decided to give the self analysis a rest and go to bed.

Returning to the house, I noticed that Turk had disappeared, and so I went back to the garden, calling his name. Ahead of me, silhouetted by the dying flames of the fire, Turk stood alert, staring into the fire and growling. The growling developed into a bark as he ran to and fro, all the while focused on the fire pit. As I came nearer, it became clear that Turk's attention was not drawn to the fire itself, but to something – or someone – on the other side of the fire pit. I moved a few paces to the left, the better to see who or what had so perturbed the dog, and saw a shadowy figure at the edge of the lawn under the beeches. Reasoning that one of the pickers had lingered in the vineyard before going to bed, I whistled the dog and called him to heel. When I looked again for the dark figure, he – or she – had disappeared into the trees. Turk's hackles, like the hairs on the nape of my neck, rose. I remembered the moonlit palm trees at the casino and that inexplicable feeling of being watched.

'Okay, Turk,' I said. 'Let's go to bed.'

Vendredi 16 Séptembre 2011

I was first up.

I'd settled up with the grape pickers before the méchoui last night, and now their caravan of shabby vehicles – a couple of old 205s, an ancient minibus and a rusty old Citroën H van – was ready to move north to John Clare's place. We said our goodbyes, sad to be parting but looking forward to our next reunion in twelve months' time. A winemaker's life is marked by these annual events, a tree-ring pattern of harvests – wet, late, perfect, disastrous – all etched into the memory. Lately, the years seem to pass so quickly. I wondered what events might mark the coming year and what part, if any, Pierre Lefèvre might play in them.

I called John to tell him the pickers were on their way. I told him, too, about the identity of the bearded man, Grouazel, and about Pierre's warning to be vigilant. John told me not to worry, but to call him any time for the least reason. I offered to help him with his harvest, but he refused and invited me, along with Wendy, Archie and Loubna, to dine at Domaine du Soleil after the work was finished, early the following week. He was hopeful that Hakim could be there too.

The day was spent clearing up after the previous evening's celebrations, monitoring the temperature of the fermentation vats, and – for me – worrying about the ceremony, coming up in two days' time, for which I felt far from prepared. This year, the world's media would be more than usually interested in the Jurade: a Hollywood actor and billionaire vineyard owner was to be elected to the inner council. Even I recognised the chisel-jawed, steely-eyed film star, famous for his romantic and crime-fighting roles. Archie and Loubna were clearly jealous that I would be dining with one of their movie heroes; Wendy pretended not to know the man. I promised them I'd ask for his autograph.

Sure, I was excited about the event, especially as Pierre would be accompanying me, but my anxieties, as usual, would trouble me all weekend.

After lunch we received a new batch of Tronçais oak barrels, which Archie and I checked and installed before cleaning and sterilizing those from the previous two years. He'd planned to make some deliveries in Bergerac, but by the time we'd finished in the barrel store it was nearly seven p.m. and Loubna and Wendy had prepared supper. After yesterday's feasting it was a sober affair, and even Wendy kept off the booze for once. Archie bolted his food, then set off in the 4x4, leaving the rest of us to do the washing up.

Once the dishes were done, Loubna came with me and Turk for an early evening stroll through the vineyard and down to the valley as far as the railway line. Dark clouds gathered in the western sky somewhere over the rivers towards the Médoc. In the dimming light, shorn of their fat bunches of ripe black grapes, the vines looked bare and forlorn. But they'd done their duty, given me fifteen thousand litres of juice – enough to keep Fontoube in business for another year, assuming I could sell the wine.

My mood, too, was somewhat forlorn; a melancholy due, no doubt, to fatigue. Loubna, I sensed, was also not her usual happy self. I wondered if she felt homesick.

'Missing home?' I asked, flashing her a friendly smile.

She scanned the horizon – a sea of vines topped by the ridge of the côte and the clear blue sky beyond. 'I miss the light,' she said quietly.

'It must be very different in Morocco.'

'Yes, the golden light of the sun, the white light of the moon, the crystal light of the water in the mountain streams. It makes me sad to think about home. You have sunshine in Saint-Emilion, but often the clouds here are dark and heavy. Dark days make me feel sad.'

'I understand, Loubna. I get like that too, even on sunny days.'

She fixed me with her gorgeous green eyes.

'Even when there are no clouds?'

'Sometimes the clouds are inside you,' I said.

The green eyes held me. 'God will send away the clouds and replace them with the light of his love.'

We'd just turned round to go back to the château when I heard the distant rumble of a diesel motor and the sound of tyres on the gravel. We listened as the vehicle turned on the drive, and I wondered whether the driver was lost, doubling back to continue their journey; but, no, the engine had stopped.

'Sounds like we might have a customer, Loubna.'

The two of us walked, a little more quickly now, back to the house. We were almost at the courtyard when a second vehicle arrived – a dark blue saloon. Business is brisk today, I thought. But this second visitor was not there to buy wine. I recognised the car and its driver: it was Pierre. He pulled up, blocking the gate, and cut the engine. Then, rather than coming to greet us in his usual friendly manner, he hesitated before opening the door and got out cautiously. By now I could see the other vehicle: a white Mercedes van. A big, bearded North-African man was sitting at the wheel, staring through the windscreen at Pierre.

Turk let out a nervous growl.

Pierre shouted to the man: 'Remove the keys and step out of the cab.' Then to us: 'Stay back!'

He watched Loubna and me retreat to the first row of

vines, gestured to us to keep down, then continued slowly towards the van. We took cover, catching glimpses of the action through the foliage. I held Turk in my arms, my heart beating in time with the little dog's rapid panting. Once again, Pierre ordered the driver to get out of the cab, then moved forward another couple of paces and out of our line of sight. Loubna looked at me questioningly, but I could offer no words of reassurance or explanation. All was calm. Even the rooks in the chestnuts were silent. A cricket in the coarse grass beyond the vines stopped chirruping. Seconds passed, then the silence was broken by a diesel engine coughing into life and the sound of tyres spinning in the gravel. I dropped the dog and ran out of the vines, closely followed by Loubna.

What I witnessed, there in the courtyard, will stay with me forever.

Pierre stood midway between his Peugeot and the van, a distance of perhaps thirty metres. The van's wheels had stopped slipping in the gravel and were now propelling the vehicle at speed towards Pierre, who appeared to be struggling with something at his belt. He put out his hand, almost defensively, just as the van reached his position. He stepped to the side, but the van swerved towards him, clipped his shoulder and span him, head over heels, face-down on the ground. The driver applied the brakes too late, sending the van skidding head-on into Pierre's car. I heard the crunch of the collision and a dull thud as the driver's head hit the windscreen.

A moment later the bearded man stumbled from the cab clutching a butcher's knife, and staggered towards Pierre.

'Take Turk to the house,' I whispered to Loubna, 'lock yourself in and look after Wendy. Go!'

What I did next took me completely by surprise. As Loubna ran to the side entrance, hefting the dog, I took the first of several reluctant steps towards Pierre and his assailant.

'Leave him alone!' I shouted.

The man, by now two strides from the captain's motionless body, turned and stared at me. Covered, as it was, with blood from a broad gash on his forehead, I knew his face nonetheless. This was the man we'd seen at the sulphur factory. This was René Rougeard's killer. This was Abdul Grouazel, and he'd come here for me, not Pierre Lefèvre.

After a moment's hesitation he turned, wiped his bloodied face with his sleeve, and jogged drunkenly in my direction muttering curses and wielding the knife.

I ran.

I know my vines – every trunk, shoot and tendril. My vines could save me from the attacker. I sprinted along the rows hoping to gain enough distance to lose him in the maze of cabernets and merlots. But, by God, he was fast. Tall, strong and determined, despite his injury, he would surely outrun me. By the time I reached the first of the young vines on the lower slopes he'd gained on me, his curses sounding louder, his footsteps pounding on the heavy soil. If only I could find something to defend myself with – a wooden trellis stake perhaps, a mallet, or my pneumatic secateurs – then perhaps I could save my skin until Pierre's colleagues arrived. Who was I kidding! There was only one thing I could do: I kept on running.

He was two paces behind me. A vine root snared my left foot and sent me tumbling and sprawling to the ground. I was helpless, done for, almost ready to submit to the man's grisly intentions – almost. I rolled onto my back, squirming away from his grasp, and kicked out with both feet. My right heel connected with his groin, and for a few breathless moments, my attacker retreated one, two steps, then stooped, clutching a trellis wire, and spat. I scrabbled to my feet and made it as far as the middle of the next vine row before I felt his hot breath on the back of my neck. A terrible hand clawed at my hair, clamped me in a vice-like fist. I fell to my knees like a quivering vine shoot, a whimpering, frightened child. The fist tugged my head back revealing to me a beautiful sky of deep, peaceful

143

blue. I felt the blade's cold metal edge on my larynx, closed my eyes . . .

Then I heard an urgent, confident voice.

'Put the knife down!'

I was hoisted to my feet and spun round. At the far end of the row stood Loubna, silhouetted before the westering sun, feet apart, shoulders back, clasping a pistol with both hands and aiming dead straight at Grouazel and me. At her heels, Turk lingered obediently, growling.

'I said, put the knife down!'

Unable to move, let alone speak, I watched the scene unfold – a passive bystander, a helpless hostage with no means of escape.

Slowly, we shuffled backwards, away from Loubna and the gun. The knife pressed harder against my flesh. I looked at my dear little dog. His growls progressed to a crazed barking. I don't know why, but something told me my assailant was afraid of dogs. Turk's patience ran out. He took two cautious steps, and then raced towards us yapping and snarling, showing his fangs. He made straight for Grouazel's right leg and sank his sharp little teeth into the man's Achilles tendon. Grouazel let out a roaring scream, and I grappled with the arm that held the knife. Attempting to defend himself against the dog's attack, he released his grip on my hair, and I scrambled on all fours to the end of the row. Desperate to escape to the safety of the house but reluctant to desert my friends, I lay there among the foliage, watching. Grouazel slashed wildly at Turk, who battled valiantly and then yelped and disappeared into the vines. The man paused to consider his next move. Oh, God, I thought, not Loubna!

I watched, horrified, as he limped away from me, towards the girl, still clutching a knife as long as my forearm. She screamed, but there was no fear in her voice.

'PUT THE KNIFE DOWN NOW OR I WILL BLOW YOUR FUCKING BRAINS OUT!'

For the first time Grouazel spoke.

'You are not going to shoot me, *mademoiselle*.'

He quickened his pace, raised the knife above his head.

Three shots rang out across the valley, each one succeeded by its echo from the limestone côte above the vineyard. Three shots that stunned the birds again to silence, stilled the noisy insects. Three shots, followed by the distant wail of a police siren.

Grouazel had fallen on his back. Loubna, standing over him, the gun aimed at his gory head, kicked each of his legs then put her hand to his throat. I approached her, stunned, as yet unable to speak. Looking at me with gorgeous, baleful eyes, she whispered, 'And so unto God are all affairs returned.'

With some effort I managed to speak. 'Bloody Hell, Loubna, are you okay?'

She smiled. 'Yes, Jeanne. You?'

'I...I think so.' I wanted to hug her, but she was still holding the gun. 'Where did you get *that*?'

'From the captain.'

'Oh, God, Pierre!'

I turned and ran, out of the vines and back up the slope, hoping – praying even – that Pierre was alive. Loubna followed, calling to me, but her words were masked by the increasing noise of the sirens. When I reached the courtyard, two Libourne police squad cars had arrived at the gate. Wendy, sitting on the ground beside Pierre's supine form, cradled the man's head in her lap while attempting to stop Turk licking his face. Loubna and I approached this bizarre tableau; she took control of the dog, checking him for injuries, and I knelt in the gravel next to Pierre.

'Don't worry, dear,' Wendy said, calmly. 'Loubna saw to him, didn't you my gorgeous?'

'Yes, he's okay, Jeanne,' Loubna said. 'I was trying to tell you. I put him in the recovery position. He's out cold. I think he banged his head.'

At that moment, I knew I would give my life to save

Pierre's, because mine would serve no purpose without him. I thought of the three men I'd loved and lost. I would not lose this one. Not now, not ever.

'Pierre,' I sobbed, kissing his pallid face. 'Don't leave me. I need you. I love you!'

After the ambulance had departed, bound for the hospital in Libourne, we'd each been interviewed separately in the salon by a uniformed policewoman. I had countless questions of my own, but the officer had been reluctant to tell me too much. I would have to wait until the morning to speak with Pierre personally.

Later, at the oak table in the kitchen, with a recently emptied brandy glass in one hand and a mug of hot tea in the other, my state of mind began to settle. Loubna, Wendy and the uniformed officer were staring at me. I sensed that someone had asked a question to which I was expected to respond.

Wendy spoke. 'She asked you where he is, Jeanne. Where's Archie?'

'Oh, sorry, I was miles away,' I replied, turning to the kindly, concerned face of the uniformed officer. 'He's out doing deliveries in the 4x4. Should be in Bergerac by now – the Lion d'Or, then the Hôtel du Pont.'

'Can you call him, Madame Valeix?'

'Er, no, he won't use a mobile – something to do with microwaves . . .'

'Okay,' she said, glancing through the open door. 'If you tell me the car's registration I'll get someone to fetch him before I go off duty.'

'It's 1314 AM 33. I'm sure there's no need though, unless . . . He's not in danger is he?'

Again, the officer smiled. 'No, *madame*, I think the danger has . . . passed.' She looked at Loubna, then rose from her seat. 'They'll let him know about all this, and make sure he gets home safely. I'm afraid your courtyard is a crime scene now, and the boys will be busy here for the rest of the night. Good evening, *mesdames*.'

'Thank you,' I said. 'Good evening.'

The three of us sipped our tea, then joined hands across the table like the participants in a séance. I was the first to speak.

'Loubna, you are a remarkable young woman. You were so brave!'

'No, you saved the captain's life, Jeanne. You are the one who is brave.'

Brave? My actions, I knew, were motivated by blind, ignorant panic, not bravery. 'Nonsense,' I said, 'you saved mine.'

'And Turk, of course,' Wendy said, bending down to stroke the ears of the dog curled up at her feet. 'You helped, didn't you boy!'

'Yes, brave little Turk . . . and you, too, Wendy. You stayed with Pierre.'

I stared at the empty glass goblet, ran a fingertip round the rim until it rang. I needed some answers.

'Loubna, how did you do it? I mean, what happened?'

She stared at me. 'As I told the policewoman, I went indoors, asked Wendy to dial 112, made sure she and Turk were safe, then went out to help Captain Lefèvre. I checked his pulse and his breathing, turned him on his side, took his SIG from his belt . . .'

'His—?'

'His SIG Saur pistol, Jeanne.'

'You . . . certainly seemed to know how to use it.'

'A friend of mine at the gun club has one.'

'The gun club? You're a member of a gun club?'

'Yes, Jeanne, I go with my grandfather. As he always says "Morocco is God's country, but there are devils there too."'

I drained my cup.

'But the way you spoke to him! You were incredible!'

Loubna blushed. 'Yes, I am sorry for the bad language. My grandfather also says that death arrives like an eagle, silently. He says that where there is shouting and cursing, there's usually less killing. I tried shouting, but when that didn't work I tried shooting. Shooting worked.'

'I see. Well, thank God for that.'

'Yes, thanks be to God.

Wendy, who until then had been uncharacteristically restrained, squeezed my hand and said, 'I overheard the police talking in the courtyard, Jeanne. Pierre knew that you were in danger. He knew that that man out there was coming to get you!'

'Wendy,' I said, 'is there any of that cognac left?'

Samedi 17 Séptembre 2011

I'd called the *hôtel de police* the previous evening; thankfully Pierre was doing fine. They were treating him for concussion and a dislocated shoulder at Libourne hospital, and he would probably be discharged in the morning.

I woke up later than usual, showered quickly and put on my best, tightest jeans and a white cotton blouse. I took my time applying my makeup – eager to see Pierre, but wanting to look my best. I finished with a double dose of No.5 and hurried downstairs. A clear cobalt sky betokened another hot day. I considered driving into town with the roof down, but decided, for my hair's sake, against it. Nothing could have tempted me to eat; my stomach would accept only a coffee – strong, black and sweet – which I gulped down at the kitchen table as the grandfather clock chimed nine.

It's not easy to break the speed limit in a Citroën 2CV but, by God, I tried, and arrived at the hospital twenty minutes later. The news kiosk in the foyer kept Pierre's daily paper, but no flowers, grapes or cards. *Le Figaro* would have to do. An officer escorted me to Pierre's room and held open the swing door. Bright sunlight, filtering through a vase of helianthus on the windowsill, filled the room with a peaceful yellow glow. My phobia of hospitals and the musty smell of the flowers mixed with the unmistakable odour of TCP made me queasy. A pretty young nurse, preoccupied with Pierre's pillows, nodded to me as I entered.

'*Bonjour*,' I said. 'Nice flowers.'

'From my sister,' Pierre said. '*Lemon Queen*, apparently.'

The pretty nurse stopped fussing, walked past me to the door and pushed it open. 'I'll leave you and your husband to have a chat,' she said. 'Back in five minutes, okay?'

'Okay,' Lefèvre replied, 'but she's not—'

The door swung shut, and we were alone.

'Jeanne, how are you? They told me you were attacked – are you okay?'

'I'm fine, Pierre. Don't worry about me.'

'I do worry about you,' he said, patting the bedcovers by his side.

I sat on the edge of the bed and gave him a warm, caring smile.

'So, feeling better?' I asked, passing him the newspaper.

He thanked me, rummaged on the bedside table for his reading glasses, then sank back on his pillow and sighed.

'Jeanne,' he began, in a tone that suggested a negative reply was on the way. 'I have disobeyed my superior, made an enemy of the future mayor, failed to draw my side-arm against a suspected murderer, got myself knocked unconscious during a pursuit, then allowed a young Moroccan girl to take my gun and shoot dead the one remaining suspect in the case. If I were not in hospital and didn't have the worst headache of my life, I would say that things are as bad as they could be. As it is, I wish someone would shoot *me*.'

I maintained the sincere bedside manner and stroked his hair.

'Pierre . . .' I said, 'Do you recollect what I said to you yesterday, just before they put you in the ambulance. And do you remember what I *did*?'

I gazed at his puppy dog eyes. He remembered alright.

'The kiss?' he said, smiling. 'Yes, I think I do remember.'

'Good. So there's no need to feel so glum, is there?'

He shook his head.

'Jeanne,' he said, 'would you say it again? Would you *do* it again?'

I would, of course. And so I did.

We spent five very enjoyable minutes together on the hospital bed until footsteps approached the door and in came the nurse with Pierre's discharge papers and a suspicious but complicit look on her pretty face.

Pierre coughed and said, '. . . so, unless I can get some charges to stick, I won't just be off the case – I'll be off the force. Thank God Dauzac is back at work.'

Just then the door swung open again and in came Pierre's lieutenant, Dauzac. This wasn't the first time the three of us had been together in a hospital room; last time I was the one in the bed. On that occasion Pierre had ticked me off for putting myself at risk, but Dauzac had been so sweet, so gentle. I had not forgotten his friendly, intelligent eyes, the charcoal colour of his lips, his smooth ebony skin, and, in his voice, that just-detectable trace of his East-African homeland. He was six feet tall, very good looking and as gay – as the French say – as a seal.

'Well, speak of the devil!' Pierre said. 'Welcome back, Dauzac. I'm sorry you missed all the fun!'

We exchanged glances.

'*Bonjour, capitaine*,' he said, adding, 'Madame Valeix, it's nice to see you.'

'And it's good to see you too,' I said.

'So, what has my lieutenant got for me, then?'

'We found the files and the computer in Grouazel's van.'

Pierre's supercilious expression melted into one of pure joy. 'Good work, *mon gars*, good work! Now, get me out of here – we have a case to prepare.'

While we waited in the corridor for Pierre to get dressed

and collect his things, Dauzac and I chatted amiably about his holiday in Mauritius and my harvest at Fontloube. The captain emerged looking slightly dishevelled, and together we made our way down to the hospital's main doors. In the time it took to go from the ward to the car park, I was able, at last, to piece together some of the actions and motives that had led to yesterday's gruesome events.

'Okay, Dauzac,' Pierre said, 'tell me everthing.'

'Forensics matched Grouazel's DNA to hairs found at the murder scene.'

'Good, what about Hakim Watar?'

'After making a positive id of Grouazel's body this morning, he was released.'

'Good work. What have we got on Lemaitre?'

'Not much. Foliot has the files and the computer equipment in his office.'

'*Merde!* Has he put together a team? Are the technos involved?'

'Nothing yet. He just got back from the South of France. And he doesn't seem to be in much of a hurry – too busy claiming the credit for Grouazel.'

'*Mon dieu!* That man is lower than a rat's balls.' Pierre stopped, rubbed his shoulder. 'Sorry, Jeanne,' he said.

'Look, Pierre, Lieutenant, could you please tell me what happened? I mean how—?'

Pierre moved his hand from his shoulder to mine. 'Jeanne, I went to the casino yesterday, and told Lemaitre about the dossier. He was . . . edgy, red in the face, sweating like a bull. But he denied La Girondine's illegal activities, refused to cooperate, and threatened to have me dismissed if I continued my inquiries. Oddly, when I asked him if he employed a tall, heavily built North African at his factory, he looked like he'd seen a phantom. "Foliot is dealing with that," was all he would say. As I was leaving he said another odd thing: "Look, Lefèvre," he said, "Tell that *vigneronne* of yours to be vigilant." On the way back I called-in and found out that Foliot's men were on a stakeout in Bassens. I knew then that you were in danger, Jeanne, real danger.'

'How did Foliot find out about him?' I asked. 'Had he worked out the link with the factory, too?'

'He's not that clever,' Dauzac said.

'Show some respect for your commandant, Dauzac!' Lefèvre said, smiling. 'At first I thought that maybe he'd worked it out – the lab report confirmed there was sulphur on the overalls – but Foliot couldn't have got it that quickly. Then I thought of Foliot's father-in-law, his agitation, his reaction to my question about the factory and the recent breakthrough in the case . . . Then it came to me: what if the North African was threatening Lemaitre, and Lemaitre had gone to his son-in-law for help? I was not confident that Foliot would catch Grouazel before he got to you.'

'But why me?' I asked. 'Why did he come to Fontloube?'

'He saw you at the sulphur factory. He knew you were onto him. You could identify him, I suppose. Perhaps the hunter did not like being hunted. What do we have on him, Dauzac?'

Dauzac flipped open a notepad. 'Abdul Grouazel, bodyguard, thirty-six, French citizen born in Tunis, convictions for abduction and extortion, wanted in connection with a couple of violent crimes in his hometown of Marseille, known to our colleagues there and to his clients as Le Boucher. Apparently he came from a family of halal butchers.'

I tried not to think about the butcher's knife, cold against my skin. 'How did he know where to find me?'

'I don't know. I have a terrible feeling that Foliot and Lemaitre may have to answer that question . . . '

I shuddered. 'Will you question them? Arrest them?'

Pierre looked pensive. 'Well, Lemaitre is the company's *directeur generale*. It might be enough . . . No, it's hopeless, our only witnesses are dead. Without them we need written proof!'

I considered Pierre's predicament. Why should I care about Lemaitre's fate? You might say that, for me, justice had been done – in my vineyard the previous evening. Again I shuddered, remembering Hakim Wattar's words: *the case will already be judged.* On the other hand, it was my duty to do everything I could to bring the scam's mastermind to justice. Business is tough enough for winemakers like John Clare and me without corporate fraudsters manipulating the market and destroying our reputation. Above all, my devotion to Pierre meant that I had to help him. His case was far from watertight: if the only evidence against Lemaitre was circumstantial, a jury might side with this respected Bordeaux businessman, believing he was ignorant of his company's nefarious activities. Pierre needed proof of Lemaitre's role in the wine fraud, and perhaps even Rougeard's death which, I had to admit, bothered me – the last thing I needed was to be dragged into another murder trial.

'Tell me one thing, Pierre,' I said. 'Why did Abdul Grouazel kill Rougeard? Do you think Lemaitre arranged some sort of execution?'

'No, that's one thing I do not believe he is capable of. My guess is that he told Grouazel to steal the computer and the files linked to La Girondine, and give Rougeard a bloody good fright. Looks like he did both, and worse . . . No, a murder conviction may be out of the question, but I'm going to nail Lemaitre with the fraud charge if it's the last thing I do.'

Well, here goes, I thought: 'It strikes me you need an expert witness, Pierre. Someone who knows the case. Someone with experience in the wine trade. A member of the Jurade, for example?'

'Jeanne,' Pierre said, opening the rear door of Dauzac's 308, 'get in the car.'

Dauzac drove, and Pierre and I sat in the back. 'We have to get access to those files,' said Pierre. 'Where's the chief?'

'He's in Saint-Emilion checking security for tomorrow.'

'Ah, yes, the big event. Good, that just leaves Foliot. Jeanne, have you got your phone with you?'

'Yes, Pierre,' I said, adding sarcastically, 'and the battery is charged.'

'Okay, call Foliot. Say that Grouazel told you something about the wine scam but you don't want to discuss it over the phone. Do you think you can do that?'

'You want me to commit perjury?'

'Yes.'

'What's the number?'

He took my phone and punched in Foliot's mobile number, then passed it back to me, ringing.

'Foliot,' a voice said.

'Commandant Foliot? This is Jeanne Valeix speaking.'

'*Ah, bonjour, madame.* How are you feeling? I have just flown back from Nice – sorry I was not able to see you last night.'

'Oh, please don't apologise. And I am fine, thank you.'

'Good, good. Is there something I can assist you with?'

'Well, yesterday evening, that man said something to me . . .'

'Grouazel? Your assailant?'

'Yes. He was talking about some sort of wine fraud . . .'

'Madame Valeix, what exactly did he say to you?'

I put on my confused and vulnerable voice. 'I'm not sure I remember clearly . . .'

'Please, don't upset yourself. I will come and see you if that is convenient? Are you at home?'

'Yes,' I lied.

We parked a couple of blocks from the *hôtel de police* and walked over to the public gardens. On the way I called

155

Wendy to warn her of the commandant's arrival and to ask her to make my excuses. Pierre, Dauzac and I hid behind the war memorial opposite the station, peeking out at the front entrance from time to time like characters in a Tex Avery cartoon. After only a few minutes Foliot appeared on the pavement followed by Jonzac. They jumped into an unmarked car parked in front of the station and hared off along Cour Tourny.

'Let's go,' said Pierre.

I was back again at the *hôtel de police*. From the front desk on the ground floor to Pierre's office on the second, I lost count of the number of back-slappings and mickey-takings he received from his fellow officers, and the praises and kind words of concern they reserved for me. The squad room was hectic. The captain had screwed up, but certain facts warranted a celebration: a colleague had escaped a potentially fatal assault, an innocent victim had been saved, and – best of all – the bad guy had got what he deserved. It was a relief to leave the hubbub behind the closed the door of Foliot's office. On a small table sat a desktop computer, plugged into a printer and a screen which displayed a slide-show of Rougeard's vineyards. Next to the table was a stack of box files four feet high.

'Okay, Dauzac, you check the emails on the computer and Jeanne and I will go through the paper files.' He looked at his watch. 'We have no more than forty minutes.'

Dauzac sat down in front of the screen and brought up Rougeard's email list. I took a folder from the pile and saw at once the name of S.A.S. La Girondine on the first document – a sales invoice from April 2008. The other files, too, contained sales orders, collection receipts, invoices and money transfers, all relating to the same wine company. Just as Loubna had said, Rougeard was getting a very good price for his wine and it was increasing steadily year on year.

'How are you getting on, Dauzac?' Pierre asked.

'Lots of order confirmations—'

'But is Lemaitre named?'

'We've got plenty of emails from La Girondine, but nothing with Lemaitre's name on it.'

'There has to be something. Rougeard knew what was going on. He must have had some written proof, otherwise how would he have blackmailed Lemaitre? Grouazel stole these files, so the proof must be in them.'

Again, he checked the time.

'*Merde*, Foliot could be back in fifteen minutes. Jeanne, do you see anything?'

'He kept a tidy filing system. All I've found looks perfectly innocent – apart from the crazy prices he was being paid.'

We continued sifting through the pile of papers, desperately scanning each page, hoping to find something, *anything*, with Lemaitre's name on it. Dauzac, after running a search for La Girondine, tried searches with other key words – Lemaitre, MidWest, Jefferson's Cellar – but with no result. With ten minutes to go before Foliot's expected return I decided to call Archie, the only computer expert I know.

Hoping he'd be at home, I dialled Fontloube, and he picked up. I told him what we were trying to do and turned on the phone's loudspeaker. After some discussion about personal email accounts, internet histories and password caches, Archie and Lieutenant Dauzac had managed to get access to a second email system. A few clicks later and Dauzac's serious frown relaxed into a satisfied grin. 'That's it,' he said, 'we're in.'

'Thanks Archie,' I said. 'I have to go now.'

'There was a policeman here looking for you, Jeanne.'

'Yes, I know. Don't worry, I'll be home soon.'

'Okay.'

I cut the call, leaving the phone switched on, and looked again at Dauzac's smiling face. 'Something interesting?'

'*Ouais*,' Dauzac said, turning the screen towards me. The email's subject caught my eye: Bonjour Victor!

De: f.degeulle@lagirondine.fr

Date: vendredi, 20 février, 2009 15:26
A: rene.rougeard@hotmail.fr
Sujet: Tr: Tr: Re: Bonjour Victor!
Pièce jointe : girondine.se.xls

azerty

— — — — Original message — — — —
De: vlemaitre58@wanadoo.fr
Date: mercredi, 18 février, 2009 16:03
A: f.degeulle@lagirondine.fr
Sujet: Tr: Re: Bonjour Victor!
Pièce jointe : girondine.xls

Frank,
Voici le tableau. Je te laisse parler aux producteurs. Comme tu peux le constater la demande est assez élevée.
A bientôt.
VL.

— — — — Original message — — — —
De: vlemaitre58@wanadoo.fr
Date: Mercredi, 18 février, 2009 08:55
A: cdavidson@midwestbrewers.com
Sujet: Re: Bonjour Victor!
Pièce jointe : girondine.xls

Dear Chuck,
So nice to hear from you. We are all here delighted to learn that MidWest will renew the contract for the Jeffersons Cellar collection. The details of the provisions (joined) show the volumes and prices we

158

agreed. I am happy to say that we can
fulfil the order as requested, and the
future uplift in accordance with your
growth projections.
How kind of you to remember our little
family party. I will pass on your regards
to Sophie, and please pass on ours to
Margaret. Thank you for the invitation,
after the elections we would be delighted
to come. And you must both come over to
Bordeaux for the summer festivals.
Looking forward to seeing you soon.
Kind regards,
Victor.

Victor Lemaitre
Président Directeur-Générale
S.A.S. La Girondine
1, Place de la Concorde
33050 Libourne

- - - - Original message - - - -
From: Chuck Davidson
(cdavidson@midwestbrewers.com)
Date:18/02/2009 9:49 PM (GMT+07:00)
To : Victor Lemaitre
Subject : Bonjour Victor!

Dear Victor,
Bonjour!
Well, it all went through like we said. The
board were delighted with your proposal. It
was a BIG ask and I would like to say how
pleased we all are with the partnership.
Ten million bottles will certainly put St-
Emilion AND your company on the map – from
sea to shining sea you might say! Can you
resend me a copy of the spreadsheet so I
can have our purchasing guys finalize the
contract? I don't have a copy on my phone.
Thanks again for such a wonderful evening's

entertainment at the Château. Margaret and
I will never forget that "soirée"!! Look us
up if you're ever in Minneapolis, or we
could host you and Sophie at the lodge in
Aspen?
Speak again soon,
Chuck.

Sent from Iphone

I was a little confused; Pierre looked even more so.

Dauzac explained: 'It's an email trail from an American called Chuck Davidson, sent to Victor Lemaitre who replied, then transferred it to someone at La Girondine called Frank Deguelle. From there it was forwarded to Rougeard.'

'I don't understand,' said Pierre. 'Why would La Girondine send that to Rougeard?'

'Look at the text,' said Dauzac, 'it's nonsense – just the first six letters on the keyboard. I don't think it was sent officially. Maybe someone hacked into La Girondine's computer and forwarded it?'

'Open the attachment.'

Dauzac clicked on the file. A table of figures filled the screen. 'Looks like a schedule of orders, the volumes to be shipped, and the price.'

'How much were they shipping in total?' I asked.

He scrolled down to the summary. 'Looks like . . . nearly seven million litres.'

Pierre was smiling from ear to ear. 'Good work, Dauzac,' he said, patting the lieutenant on the shoulder.

I was less convinced. 'But this isn't a contract, Pierre,' I said. 'Like Dauzac says, it's a schedule, a proposal. There are no signatures.'

'It's enough for now, Jeanne. Enough for the fraud squad, at least. And it was clearly enough for a successful blackmail.'

'Successful . . . up to a point,' said Dauzac.

'Quite,' said Pierre, adding, '*merde*, Folliot will be back any minute. Print that out, Dauzac, quickly, and Jeanne, you help me file these papers.'

In the flustered minutes that followed, the paper in the printer jammed and an entire box file of invoices spilled onto the floor. We'd just put the paperwork in order and finally retrieved the printouts, when a young officer came in to say that Foliot had arrived downstairs. Pierre and I fled to his own office and Dauzac was sent to his desk and told to waylay the commandant if necessary.

Once inside his office, Pierre took the printouts from me, then looked me up and down.

'You'll have to hide,' he said, breathing heavily.

'What—?'

'Quick, under the desk!'

Feeling like a second-rate actress in a West-end farce, I crawled under Pierre's desk just as the office door opened.

I squatted there on the nylon carpet amid a tangle of electrical cables, staring at Pierre's legs. I couldn't help myself: I tickled his knee, then began to stroke a tense, muscular thigh. He closed his legs, trapping my hand painfully. I might have uttered a curse had I not heard Foliot's voice above me. Though the conversation was muffled by the desk, I caught every cringe-making word.

'Ah, Lefèvre,' Foliot began. 'Have you seen that winemaker friend of yours today?'

'*Bonjour*, Commandant, how was your trip?'

'Never mind that—' He stopped himself, adding, 'By the way, how are you since the . . . accident?'

'Much better, thank you. And at least we can close the Rougeard case now—'

'No thanks to you, *capitaine*. Now, about your lady friend—' Again he stopped, and there followed an uncomfortable pause. 'Lefèvre, can you smell perfume?'

'Er, no, Commandant. Perhaps it is my aftershave?'

Another pause. 'Not unless you have started using Channel No.5?'

Oh, shit, I thought.

The silence continued except for a faint beeping sound. Just then three things happened in quick succession: my phone rang, I jumped out of my skin and bumped my head on the underside of the desk. The phone's screen displayed the number Pierre had dialled earlier: Xavier Foliot's. Faced with no alternative I emerged sheepishly from under the desk. I looked up at the stern-faced commandant, my hair a tangled mess, my cheeks as red as new wine.

'Madame Valeix,' Foliot said, 'what are you doing under the desk of Captain Lefèvre?'

I held up my phone. 'I . . . dropped this?'

Foliot looked like he was about to explode. Luckily, at that moment, the door opened and in walked a tall, grey-haired senior officer followed closely by Lieutenant Dauzac.

'Ah, Commissaire Lamarque,' Pierre said, rising to attention. 'What fortunate timing. We have some very important news on the Rougeard case.'

'Which is?' the older policeman said.

Pierre held up the printout in front of him. 'We have discovered evidence of a major fraud, a motive for the crimes committed by Abdul Grouazel, and a new suspect who we believe was an accessory to Rougeard's murder and to the attempted murder of Madame Valeix.'

I looked at Foliot's face; his eyeballs swivelled in their sockets. He appeared desperate to speak, but unable to form a sentence.

'Unfortunately, since the evidence points unequivo-cally to a member of Commandant Foliot's family, we were just about to discuss the best course of action to take.'

'Sir—' Foliot began.

'Not here Foliot,' he said, and then turned to me, smiling. 'Madame Valeix it is a pleasure to make your acquaintance. Thank you for your assistance, but we need not inconvenience you any longer. Lieutenant Dauzac here will escort you safely home, and I look forward to meeting you in more pleasant circumstances tomorrow.'

I shuffled past Pierre's desk and said my goodbyes.

'Right,' said the *commissaire*, 'you two, in my office now!'

Dauzac drove me back to the hospital car park to collect Clémentine. I expected to be asked about the encounter with Foliot, but after a little small-talk we sat in silence, watching the townsfolk of Libourne doing their Saturday shopping. I was starting to think about food when, at last, he spoke:

'You like him, don't you?'

'Who, Pierre?' I said, stalling a reply.

'*Ouais . . .*'

'Well, he's been very supportive. He's helped me a lot.'

'I mean you *like* him, no?'

'Well, yes, he's a good-looking man, I suppose – don't you think so?'

'I couldn't say. He's my boss. And he's not really my type.'

I was intrigued 'Okay, so what is your type, then?'

He thought about it. 'Honestly?'

'Honestly.'

'I prefer blondes.'

We both laughed.

'Yes, well, they say everyone has their preferred physical type.'

We took a right turn at a roundabout.

He glanced at me, smiling. 'So what's yours then?'

I didn't reply.

'Let me guess,' he said. 'Tall, late-forties, salt-and-pepper hair, chestnut eyes, eighty-five kilos?'

'Sounds good,' I said, 'go on.'

'Wears a uniform, needs a shave, good sense of humour?'

'What do you mean? He has one, or I'll need one?'

Again we laughed, and Dauzac suffered a minor coughing fit.

We arrived at the car park and pulled up in front of the 2CV.

'Seriously, do you think he'll be alright?' I asked.

Dauzac considered the question, cleared his throat. 'If he can bring this off, they'll probably make him *commissaire* of some nice seaside resort. If not, he'll probably lose his job.'

I wondered if Pierre had what it took to be a winemaker – and decided he didn't. Then I tried to imagine life in a beach-front villa, hosting dinner parties for the local well-to-dos, gardening, painting, taking bracing early morning swims . . . I couldn't see it somehow.

My kind-hearted driver sensed his passenger's disquiet. 'Don't worry, Madame Valeix. I think everything will work out fine.'

I released the seatbelt, opened the door an inch. 'Thank you, Dauzac,' I said, 'Call me Jeanne, okay?'

'Okay, Jeanne. And I am Kelile.'

'Kelile – what a lovely name.'

'It means protector.'

'Ah, and very apt too – for your job, I mean.'

'*Ouais*, Jeanne, you might say so.'

Dauzac, as instructed by his chief, followed me home, and it was gone two o'clock when we arrived at Fontloube. After introducing him to my houseguests, he made his excuses, and left me to face a barrage of questions from the others. Wendy wanted to know the identity of the smarmy police commandant who'd been looking for me earlier (she's a good judge of character), and Archie was anxious to find out if the email account had revealed anything interesting. Loubna asked me how Pierre was, and whether her dossier regarding Lemaitre and Rougeard had been useful to him. They all wanted to know about the dead man in the vineyard. I was standing next to the kitchen table, still holding the car keys, attempting to answer these questions and more when Wendy asked if I'd had anything to eat.

'Not since last night, Wendy, no.'

'Then sit down before you fall down, gorgeous girl, and I will bring you something – I think there are a few salad leaves left over from lunch.'

While Wendy busied herself between the larder and the fridge, the rest of us sat at the table, and I gave a summary of the day's events. My friends' responses ranged from shocked disbelief that Victor Lemaitre could have led a deranged killer to our door, to uncontrollable laughter when I related the embarrassing incident in Pierre's office. By the time I'd finished, Wendy had served me a large salad bowl heaped with mixed leaves, thin strips of golden-fatty smoked duck breast, several plump *gésiers de canard* and a big slice of *foie gras*.

'Eat,' she said.

'Mm, *salade landaise* – my favourite. Thank you, Wendy.'

Then she passed me a large glass of red wine.

'Drink,' she said.

'What would we do without you, Wendy?'

'Oh, I'm sure you'll cope when I'm gone.'

'By the way,' I said, my mouth full of salad, 'what did you say to Commandant Foliot?'

'I told him you'd gone to the hairdressers.'

'Gosh, did he believe you?'

'He said there were more important matters that you should be attending to.'

'What did you say to that?'

'I said it is a great thing to do what is necessary before it becomes essential and unavoidable.'

Loubna, who seemed somewhat confused by our exchanges, asked, 'Are you going somewhere, Wendy?'

Wendy gazed at the girl adoringly. 'We're all going somewhere, dear – one day.'

What's up with her? I wondered. Before I could ask, the phone rang, and I ran to the study to answer it.

'Jeanne, it's Pierre.'

'Pierre, how was it? I mean, with the chief.'

'We need some more information – lots of it. Have you got a pen?'

I rummaged in the desk drawer and pulled out a biro. 'Yes, fire away.'

'Okay, we need to know how much Saint-Emilion wine was produced each year for the past three years. Then we need everything you can find out about its distribution – the domestic market, the export market, how much was sold direct or to supermarket chains or to companies like La Girondine. Can you do that?'

'Well, yes, of course. But what did Lamarque say? What's happening?'

'The chief is on our side, Jeanne. But before we interview Lemaitre or refer any of this to the organised crime boys, he just wants to be sure.'

'Okay. What about Foliot?'

'He's refusing to answer questions until his lawyer arrives from Paris. But it doesn't look good for him.'

'What do you mean?'

'Any collusion with Lemaitre and he will face criminal charges – if he had information regarding the killer's identity, if he planted or withheld evidence, if he has any links to the wine fraud. And if we can prove he supplied your address to anyone connected with the attack – well, God help him.'

The thought that a policeman might have deliberately put our lives at risk chilled me. Then I remembered my encounter with Lemaitre outside the town hall.

'But Lemaitre had my address, Pierre. I gave him my business card last week when I saw him in Saint-Emilion – you remember, after we met at the King's Tower?'

'Jeanne, keep that to yourself for the moment, okay?'

'Okay. So what about Lemaitre?'

'If you can bring me those figures, I think we can convince the chief to grant an arrest.'

'No problem – give me an hour or so?'

'D'accord, à tout à l'heure.'

'A tout à l'heure.'

I hung up. 'Loubna,' I shouted down the hall, 'I need your help!'

After three quarters of an hour Loubna had collated the figures Pierre needed from various internet sources, and confirmed what we already knew: that MidWest's distribution of Saint-Emilion Grand Cru amounted to more than the wine's entire export market. Whatever was in the Jefferson's Cellar bottles, it certainly wasn't what it said on the label. Assuming the figures Loubna had been sent by MidWest and those referred to in the email were true, then La Girondine was passing-off thousands of hectolitres of ordinary red Bordeaux as Saint-Emilion – a fraud worth several million dollars a year.

I took the stack of pages from the printer, put them in a folder and rushed out of the house with Turk trotting after me. The drive back to Libourne gave me twenty minutes to think about my wardrobe – tomorrow's ceremonies, the parade through the town, and the banquet to be held in the Jacobin convent, all posed a problem. The forecast was for another humid day with temperatures reaching thirty degrees. Sartorial choices were limited as the red cape and hat had to be worn throughout the day, but what about shoes? A long, hot day spent traipsing the town's cobbled streets would play havoc with my feet, so sensible footwear would be the right choice. But how would I look in flat shoes, swamped in a shapeless crimson gown, a floppy red hat hiding my gorgeous curls? What had Pierre said? Ah, yes: charming.

On the other hand, if you want to drop a dress size, as the saying goes, wear heels. I pictured myself wearing a pair of perfect high heels, imagined how they would accentuate the curve of my legs, tone my calf muscles, make me appear seven pounds lighter, two inches taller and sexy as hell. Well, I could dream, and although my feet would regret it, the rest of me was happy with the decision I was about to make: after the *hôtel de police* I would pay a visit to Libourne's chicest shoe shop. That only left the question of what to do with my hair and what to wear under the gown . . .

When I got to the station, the guard on the front desk asked me to wait. Five minutes later, Pierre arrived accompanied by his chief, Lamarque.

'Hello again, Madame Valeix,' the chief said, all smiles. 'Please, come this way.'

Pierre winked at me as we went into a small meeting room, just off the foyer. We sat at a long table, the chief on one side, Pierre and me on the other. I put the folder on the table in front of me, then pushed it across to the chief.

'Thank you, *madame*,' he said, opening the folder.

'As you can see—' I began.

Lamarque held up his hand. 'Please, *madame*, allow me to read what you have so kindly brought to us.'

We waited, silently, for Lamarque to examine the papers. Pierre sat there with his fingertips pressed together, gazing up at the ceiling.

'Very interesting,' Lamarque said.

I didn't know whether to respond, so I stayed quiet.

'Perhaps, Madame Valeix, you could summarise your account of this information and that which you supplied previously to Captain Lefèvre?'

'Well, of course, although Pierre is fully aware—'

Again, Lamarque raised his right hand. '*Captaine Lefèvre* will not be conducting any further investigations in this case, involving, as it does, his superior officer and a senior public figure. I shall be handling any subsequent actions which may or may not be undertaken.'

I looked at Pierre. 'What—?'

'Commissaire Lamarque is taking over the case, Jeanne,' Pierre said.

'Ah, okay. Well. It's like this . . .'

I gave Lamarque the backstory – about Rougeard's expensive lifestyle and his links to Lemaitre. I explained my suspicion that Rougeard had been blackmailing Lemaitre – a suspicion backed up by the discovery of Rougeard's overpriced wine. Finally I told him how we'd found out that Lemaitre's company, La Girondine, was passing-off red plonk as *grand cru* wine to the Americans, who were selling it in impossibly large volumes – borne out by the data I'd brought with me.

I took a deep breath.

'Very interesting,' Lamarque said, again.

'I also believe that Lemaitre hired Gruazel to stop Rougeard blackmailing—'

Again, the raised hand. He was starting to annoy me. 'Thank you, Madame Valeix, you need not concern yourself with suppositions regarding the murder of Monsieur Rougeard.'

'Oh no? Well, what about the attempted murder of myself and Pierre?'

He looked me in the eye. 'I understand how concerned you are about your attacker's motives, but you must be patient – all will be revealed in due course.'

Well, there wasn't much left to say. 'Fine. Well, if there's nothing else I can do?'

'You have already done quite enough,' he said, forcing a smile and tapping the folder on the table. 'Once again, I look forward to speaking with you again tomorrow, at the Jurade.'

We stood, shook hands and the chief turned to leave the room.

'Lefèvre,' he said.

'*Oui, commissaire,*' Pierre replied, following his boss out into the foyer.

I stayed behind, alone, watching the door. The two men lingered outside the room, and I caught a little of what was being said:

'. . . but now we know about the investments—'

'He'll deny everything.'

'The list is quite scary, sir – fraud, perverting the course of justice, subordination of a witness, perjury, conspiracy to murder . . .'

A telephone rang at the front desk which no one seemed inclined to answer. The ringing made it difficult to hear the conversation, so I crept silently to the open door and listened to Lamarque's closing words.

'. . . a statement before we see Lemaitre. Anyway, tomorrow you go with Madame Valeix, agreed? Stick to her like glue and for God's sake don't let her do anything impulsive.'

Pierre came back into the room and the two of us nearly collided.

'Ah, Jeanne,' he said.

'What was all that about? What investments? What about tomorrow?'

Pierre looked behind him to check we were alone. 'We ran a check on La Girondine. It seems that Commandant Foliot has significant holdings in the company, all purchased in 2009.'

'Well, what a surprise!'

'Shhh! Not too loud. No one is supposed to know. We don't know if he'll cooperate, but I'm more hopeful than the chief – I know what a self-serving louse he is. Now, you go home – you must be exhausted.'

'Sure,' I said, 'but what was that he said about sticking to me like glue?'

Pierre's careworn face brightened. 'The chief wants me to accompany you during the ceremony and the banquet tomorrow – I feared that he might ask me to stay here, but—'

'What did he mean by "impulsive"?'

'Oh, don't worry about that. He just doesn't want you talking to the press, or anybody else.'

'Well, it suits me fine. I will have you all to myself tomorrow.'

'I look forward to it,' he said.

'So do I, Pierre,' I said. 'So do I.'

I gave him a peck on the cheek and hastened to the exit.

The shoe shop on Rue Gambetta is tiny, but what it lacks in size its staff make up for in haughtiness. I'd been there a few years before, but the contempt of the sales assistant – and the shocking price of the shoes – lost her the sale. This time I decided to overlook the staff's rudeness and overcome my own thriftiness. To hell with it, I said to myself as I gazed at the exquisite items in the window, you only join the Jurade once. I went indoors, selected a pair of gorgeous black heels and took them to the counter. Two sales assistants – one standing, talking on the phone; the other seated, staring at a computer screen – ignored me. In fact, they didn't even ignore me: I simply wasn't there.

I waited.

The girl on the phone continued her conversation, and her colleague remained focussed on the screen, tapping at the keyboard with long, perfectly manicured nails. The one talking on the phone had that annoying French habit of adding a nasal 'ah' sound after certain words. It's irritating as hell, and when finally she hung up and acknowledged me, I was grinding my teeth.

'*Bonjour-ah*,' she said loudly. 'May I help you *madame*?'

I showed her the shoes. 'Do you have these in other colours?'

'*Ah, oui-ah*.'

'Good. May I . . . try them?'

'What size?'

'Thirty-eight.'

She glanced at her colleague who looked up from the computer screen, pursed her glossy lips, then let out a barely audible raspberry. 'Don't know,' she said, 'I'll have to look, *d'accord-ah*?'

'Okay, I'll wait,' I said, scanning the room. Next to the computer was a copy of *Le Sud Ouest* open at a double-page feature about the Jurade. Over a photo of red-robed Jurats was a close-up picture of our famous Hollywood actor.

The computer user rose reluctantly from her seat and disappeared into a room behind the counter.

'Going anywhere nice?' the remaining assistant said disinterestedly.

'There,' I said, prodding the photo in the newspaper.

Her face brightened. '*Genial!*' she exclaimed, 'Tomorrow? When you-know-who will be there?'

I couldn't help myself: 'Yes, I'm to be inducted into the brotherhood – along with him and a dozen-or-so others.'

After a moment's reflection she looked at me doubtingly. 'It's not true, is it?'

I opened my bag and pulled out the red hat.

The hat clinched it; she could barely conceal her excitement. 'I don't know why my colleague is taking so long,' she said. 'I'll go and help her. Will you excuse me for a moment?'

Both girls returned a couple of minutes later, each bearing a stack of shoe boxes six or seven high. I was offered a seat, a cold drink and more advice than I needed concerning the wearing, storage and cleaning of hand-made shoes. They cooed and fawned like a couple of lady's maids, and after half an hour I'd tried on dozens of pairs. In the end I bought the shoes I'd first picked up when I arrived – the most expensive ones. I settled the bill, promising to mention the shop to any famous celebrity who complimented the shoes. I wouldn't, of course, but it would be nice to receive the same five-star treatment next time.

'*Au revoir-ah,*' they said in unison as I turned to leave.

Next I walked to the lingerie boutique on the corner of Gambetta and Boireau where an unusually friendly sales lady sold me a white silk two-piece which, she assured me, would please both me and Monsieur. Last of all I trotted, bags in hand, to the hair salon just before closing time. Lucky for me they managed to fit me in. Forty-five minutes later, coiffed and confident, I drove back to Fontloube, able at last to look forward to the Jurade. Barring dead bodies in wine vats and murderous knife-wielding maniacs, I was ready for anything, but, my goodness, it had been a long day.

Dimanche 18 Séptembre 2011

Turk, the poor thing, sulked. There was no room for him in the police 308 and anyway he doesn't like crowds. So while Archie distracted the little dog with a marrow bone, we filed out into courtyard, a little later than planned, to where our chauffeur awaited. Wendy, Loubna and Archie squeezed into the back. I sat in the front next to Pierre who was beautifully turned-out in his dress uniform. He kissed me on both cheeks and said I looked '*très belle*'. When I turned round to make sure everyone had fastened their seatbelts Wendy gave me a sly wink. 'Thank you, driver,' she said, 'in your own time.'

'What does she mean?' Pierre asked.

'She means step on it, Captain, we have to be at the *mairie* in five minutes.'

He gunned the engine, released the handbrake and pulled away, churning the gravel.

'Ooh, Pierre!' Wendy giggled.

'Okay,' I said, 'just get us there in one piece.'

As we swung out into the lane he gave me a cheeky smile. 'Don't worry, I am entirely committed to your safety and well-being.'

I returned the smile. 'Yes, and you're not to let me out of your sight all day, *n'est pas?*'

'All part of the job, *madame*.' he said.

The last time I'd visited Saint-Emilion's town hall I was riding a pushbike and wearing shorts and a tee-shirt. This time we arrived in style, received by two berobed footmen who opened the car doors and escorted us to the entrance. Lieutenant Dauzac, who was waiting for us on the steps, was told to park the car and take the others to the church where they would await the arrival of the procession. We turned to wave goodbye to my friends, then followed the footmen through the building and out into the formal gardens behind. I was terribly nervous and, once again, felt like an imposter as we took coffee in the gardens, rubbing shoulders with Saint-Emilion's great and good. Thankfully the morning's light drizzle provided a useful source of small-talk, and polite enquiries regarding the harvest allowed me to chat with the other *jurats* without too much stress or embarrassment. But when the owner of one of the town's most famous wineries introduced himself my hands began to tremble, causing my china coffee cup to rattle noisily on its saucer. When he asked me which grape variety would dominate this year's vintage, I nearly lost my grip and spilled half the coffee. Thankfully, my answer – that this would be a cabernet year – seemed to confirm his own view. He ordered a replacement coffee, apologised politely for startling me and welcomed me to the Jurade with a friendly smile and a warm handshake. After that I linked arms with Pierre and circulated among the guests, feeling more at ease. I recognised the film star who was chatting amiably, in passable French, with an elderly *jurat*, but something stopped me from introducing myself; autograph requests would have to wait. Pierre's chief, Comissaire Lamarque, saw me from the other side of the throng. He smiled politely, and I gave him a feeble wave.

Relax, I said to myself, don't say anything stupid or slurp you coffee and everything will be fine.

At the appointed time Lamarque addressed the gathering, speaking in the deep, authoritarian tones of a man well used to giving orders. After welcoming and thanking the organisers, members, initiates and guests, he invited everybody to follow the council members and banner bearers to the monolithic church where the

175

ceremony of oaths would begin at ten o'clock sharp.

The cortege set off along Rue Gaudet. Pierre and I followed in the rearward ranks, flattered and a little abashed by the attention of the spectators and photographers lining the cobbled streets. People cheered, red-white-and-blue flags fluttered, cameras flashed and, for the time being, my feet coped. A huddle of reporters and a mobile film crew emerged from the crowd and began calling to Pierre and me by name, firing questions at us about the attack in the vineyard. Pierre tried to repel them but they followed us as far as the Rue des Girondins where the procession turned sharp right down the narrow cobbled street. Here we were able to shake off our pursuers and continue, two-by-two, past the wine merchants and macaroon makers, the hotels and restaurants that occupy the old lane's golden-stone buildings. We turned again at Rue du Tertre and made our way down the steepest and most photographed of Saint-Emilion's streets. Half way down, my new shoes started to nip, and when we reached the medieval square by the monolithic church my feet were whingeing like a pair of travel-weary teenagers. Escaping the muggy heat outside to the sanctuary of the church was a relief. The interior of the subterranean edifice, hewn from the limestone rock of the côte, was as cool and quiet as a wine cellar. I spotted my houseguests half way down the aisle and hobbled over to them to rest my weary feet. For a few soothing minutes I was able to take off my expensive new shoes and rest awhile before being ushered to the front of the church with my fellow initiates.

I took my place, then turned round to see Wendy beaming at me, vigorously waving a copy of the order of service. Pierre, too, and the others, all gave me an encouraging wave just as the service began. Lamarque, as master of ceremonies, called out the name of each new initiate whose professional resumé was read out by a clerk. The new member then made a pledge to the Jurade before receiving their certificate with its official seal. I sat there, dreading the moment when my modest achievements would be read aloud to this exalted congregation. The Hollywood actor received his honours just before me, and when my name was called the crowd were still cheering and chattering – enough, thankfully, to drown out what the clerk said about me. I approached the dais and made my solemn vow: 'To Saint-Emilion, I am loyal.' A bell tolled twice, and I was a member of the Jurade. Pierre and my friends were still applauding enthusiastically when Lamarque moved on to the next name on the list.

After the pledges, we traipsed back up the hill to the Salle des Dominicans – the fourteenth-century Jacobin convent which was the venue for the gala luncheon. There we were served aperitifs and canapés in the gardens. My first glass of champagne since the night at the Opera went down quickly, and by the time Pierre and I had found a shady spot in which to relax, I was half way through a second glass. The little bower we'd found beneath the leafy canopy of a weeping willow gave us plenty of privacy. When no one was looking we kissed, briefly, like un-chaperoned young lovers, enjoying the thrill of teasing and being teased. All too soon, though, a waiter appeared to take our empty flutes and announce the start of lunch.

Several large round tables, dressed in white linen and laid with fine silverware and crystal glasses, had been arranged under the oak-beamed ceiling of the banqueting hall. The VIP's table – reserved for the inner council members, a couple of politicians and the film star – was set apart. At this *table d'honneur*, sat Commissaire Lamarque between a woman on his right whom I took to be his wife, and a government minister on his left. It was a pleasant enough affair, although I never truly enjoy eating on such formal occasions. However, the food, wines and service were exceptional; it's not every day you get to enjoy a dozen-or-so of Saint-Emilion's most prestigious wines with a menu created from the finest ingredients from Gascony to the Perigord. Perhaps I should have been more appreciative, but to be honest I'd have sooner stayed under the willow tree with Pierre.

Once or twice during the meal I looked up to see Lamarque staring at me. Not to be intimidated by Pierre's boss, I chatted amiably with the Master of Wine sitting next to me, and listened to Pierre and his neighbour – a grey-whiskered, senatorial wine courtesan with an infectious, endearing laugh. From time to time Pierre and I played footsie under the tablecloth and exchanged what I think they call furtive glances.

I'd just finished my dessert when, once again, I realised that I was being watched. Lamarque, fixing me with his steely gaze, whispered something to his wife who dabbed her lips on a linen napkin, patted her husband's arm and got up from her seat. She made her way towards us between the seated diners, dodging the busy waiters who were returning to the kitchen bearing armfuls of empty plates.

Pierre stood and introduced us. '*Bonsoir, madame*. This is Jeanne Valeix, owner of Château Fontloube. Jeanne, this is Madame Thérese Lamarque, the head of one of our oldest wine dynasties and the wife of Libourne's chief superintendant – my boss, that is.'

She beamed at me and we shook hands. 'Delighted to meet you, Jeanne. No, please don't get up – how are you feeling? After the attack, I mean. I couldn't believe it when my husband told me you and Pierre were both attending tonight.'

'We're fine, honestly, aren't we Pierre?'

Pierre, a little embarrassed, replied. '*Ah, oui, madame, merci.*'

Madame Lamarque sat down in Pierre's chair. 'Please accept my congratulations,' she said, still clutching my hand, still beaming. 'I've heard so many good things. You have helped Pierre to catch drugs dealers and murderers and you still have time to manage a vineyard and a winery! And you have such a beautiful complexion! Such an English rose! I don't know how you British girls stay so young-looking. You simply must tell me your secret.

Anyway, I look forward to getting to know you – will you come to the house? But, listen, we mustn't keep my husband waiting. He would very much like to speak with you – would you mind, my dear?'

'Of course not,' I said, rising.

'Good, good! And don't worry about Pierre. I will keep him company for you.'

'Thank you, Madame,' I said, and went over to Lamarque, curious to know the reason for this mysterious game of musical chairs.

'Please, do sit down, Madame Valeix,' he said.

Out of police uniform, he looked quite different from the man I'd met at the station: well-built, in pretty good shape for his age – late fifties, sixty tops – handsome, in a way, in his ermine-trimmed regalia and foppish red hat. His eyes, staring up at me from beneath bushy grey eyebrows, were serious, concerned. Oh dear, I thought, not another headmaster type. I took his wife's place and gave him my full attention. He spoke quietly, but purposefully, leaning towards me.

'Madame Valeix, I trust you have recovered after Friday's awful events?'

'Yes, thank you. I'm okay.'

'Good, good. But if you need to talk to some-body . . . we work with some excellent professionals, very good, very discrete—'

'Thank you. But, really, I'm fine.'

He paused, took a sip of water.

'Well, I'm delighted to hear it. Now, you may know that Vincent Lemaitre and Commandant Foliot have been questioned this morning and are currently under investigation by the fraud squad. Apart from Captain Lefèvre, you and I are the only people in this room who are aware of the situation. May I rely on you to keep it that way until an official announcement can be made tomorrow?'

I gave a nod of assent.

'That Libourne's future mayor and one of my own officers are involved in these woeful activities is regrettable enough, but I am also forced to admit to a personal regret. As you may know, I was the council member who proposed your investiture, mainly for your commercial successes in England – "By Appointment to Her Majesty . . . " was quite a coup, *non*? But, in part, my proposal was also a modest payback for your assistance in the Aquitaine drugs haul two years ago. It was an easy decision for me to make, and one which the council were more than happy to accept. Alas, in one way, it was a decision I regret.'

'But—' I said, scowling.

He placed his hand on mine.

'Please, please, allow me to finish. It is due to my proposal that you found yourself involved in this matter and in the dreadful events that took place at your home. And for that I offer my most sincere apologies.

'Now, once the details of this scandal are released, the media attention shown to our honoured celebrity guest here,' – he nodded towards the film star opposite us – 'will transfer to you, Madame Valeix. The glamorous English winemaker who survived an attack by the Butcher of Bassens; the beautiful chatelaine who helped solve a murder and went on to crack the biggest international wine fraud in French history. The ladies and gentlemen of the press who are with us tonight will cancel their return flights, I have no doubt. This scandal is a potentially mortal wound to Saint-Emilion's reputation and, owing to your involvement, to that of the Jurade.

'My involvement? What about Lemaitre? He was to be made a member too.'

'Was to have been, yes. Thankfully, our association with him has been somewhat mitigated. But because you uncovered the fraud, it will always be associated with the Jurade.'

'Okay,' I said. 'But that's why I'm determined to stop the fraudsters, before they can do any more damage.'

'I know, I know, and your testimony in any future proceedings will be invaluable, but the damage, I'm afraid, has already been done. However, I think we may be able turn your association with the case to our advantage'

He sighed, and filled two glasses of wine. When he replaced the bottle on its silver tray I noticed the label: Château Cheval Blanc. Sitting back in his chair, the sombre expression relaxed a little, and he passed me one of the glasses.

'As you know, the primary function of the Jurade is to promote the image of Saint-Emilion and its wines across the globe. If we are to survive – and survive we must – we will need someone of your calibre to help us. Jeanne – may I call you Jeanne? – a woman of your undoubted talents will be an invaluable asset.' He smiled at me, almost winked. 'Are we in agreement?'

Again, I nodded. 'Yes, of course, *monsieur*,' I said.

'Then welcome to the Jurade – and, please, call me Jacques.'

We chinked glasses, and I thought: how weird this is, to be here at a gala banquet attended by the world's press and one of Hollywood's biggest movie stars, sipping three-hundred euro wine with the chief of police. And he said I was glamorous. And beautiful.

I took a sip. 'My God, that's good.'

'I agree,' he said.

Superlative? Divine? Exceptional? The wine in my glass was all of these, and much more. The complex and harmonious blend of black and red fruits, liquorice, charred oak and truffle produced an irresistible bouquet. These aromas, coupled with the wine's minerality, its silky-smooth tannins and a hint of violet, gave a long, slow, mouth-watering finish. But the whole was far more mysterious than the sum of its parts. The white horse that pranced across my palate was far too elusive to be caught in a lariat of mere words. Sensations and emotions might better describe this liquid pleasure. This was a wine that made me *feel* rather than think, and the feelings it evoked were intoxicating: euphoria, ecstasy, fortitude, passion . . . In the hallowed hall of the ancient convent I had truly tasted holy wine – but my thoughts were far from chaste. When I glanced across the room at Pierre our eyes met. It was time to do something impulsive.

Madame Lamarque finished her conversation with Pierre and returned to the top table.

'Ah, Marie-Francoise, I was just saying how de-lighted we are with our new English *jurat*.'

I was still mesmerised by the sensual, almost aphrodisiac qualities of the Cheval Blanc.

'Yes, dear,' said Madame Lamarque, adding, 'but, oh, are you feeling unwell, Jeanne? It is terribly hot in the hall – would you like some fresh air?'

'What? Oh, no,' I said, 'It's just that I have a slight headache and my feet are killing me.' I showed a perfectly shod but swollen foot.

'Oh, my goodness, how on earth will you climb the King's Tower in those *talons*! You must change your shoes. Jacques will send the driver to fetch you a more comfortable pair.'

'Please,' I said, 'it's no trouble. Pierre can run me home.'

'But you have not yet had coffee!'

'That's okay, I'll pass – I think a nice cup of English tea is what I need.'

Lamarque had already beckoned Pierre who arrived at our table looking concerned.

'Ah, Lefèvre, Madame Valeix is feeling a little unwell. Would you be kind enough to escort her home?'

'Yes, sir,' Pierre replied. 'Are you alright, Jeanne?'

'It's nothing, really. I just need to pop back to Fontloube for something.' I looked up at Pierre. He alone saw the almost imperceptible twitch in my left eyebrow. With one swift movement he took out his mobile, pressed a speed-dial and put the phone to his ear. 'Dauzac,' he said, 'bring the car . . . Okay, *merci*.'

Pierre was reluctant to talk in the car, and when I asked him to relate the details of Lemaitre's and Foliot's statements he said he'd tell me later.

In twenty minutes we were back at Fontloube. Turk was so pleased to see me that he didn't even bark at Pierre. And when he saw the two of us kissing at the foot of the stairs he scurried off into the kitchen to gnaw on his bone; he's nothing if not discrete.

The kiss continued. Pierre placed his warm hands on my flushed cheeks, then gently removed the felt hat, caressed my hair, and stroked the back of my neck. I slipped off the high heels and stood on the first step, pressing myself into his embrace. His hands slid down to my behind and began to hoist the scarlet robe. I took a deep breath.

'Slow down, Pierre,' I murmured, 'what's the hurry?'

We gazed into one another's eyes. 'What about your duties at the Tower at five o'clock?' he teased.

I looked at my watch. 'It's only three-thirty, Pierre. We can take our time.'

'I am a Frenchman, Jeanne,' he whispered. 'I know how to take my time.'

'That's what I was hoping,' I said, giggling.

We were about to go upstairs when I heard the now-familiar buzzing of Pierre's phone. I gave him a disapproving look, but he took the call all the same. '*Oui,* Commissaire,' he said, taking a step down. 'Yes, Madame Valeix is fine, thank you . . . Yes, indeed, some tea . . . I understand, yes . . .'

I sat on the step in front of him, reached up to undo the zip of his navy blue trousers and slipped my hand inside.

'I'm sure she WILL—' he said, his voice climbing an octave as I gently squeezed what I held in my hand. '. . . no, it's nothing, sir, I just scalded myself on the kettle . . . yes . . . thank you, sir . . . *au revoir.*'

I took the phone from him, switched it off and said,

'Pierre, I think we are about to do something impulsive.'

Somewhat breathlessly he replied, 'Can something so long-anticipated be called impulsive?'

'I don't know, Pierre,' I said, 'but I want it – now.'

Pierre disappeared to the bathroom. While waiting for him, I took off my robes, hung them carefully in the wardrobe, then pulled back the quilt and lay on the bed dressed only in my new silk undies. I listened to the swish of the curtains billowing at the open window, enjoying the feel of the breeze on my bare arms, legs and belly. Pierre, bless him, returned from the bathroom wearing a pair of white cotton shorts, his uniform neatly folded over one arm. I smiled and checked-out his legs: tanned, toned and not too hairy. He smelled of Savon de Marseille soap and peppermint mouthwash. We kissed eagerly, then removed each other's underwear in the fumbling way new lovers do. No words were spoken. I lay back and guided him to me.

Wanton and reckless, anxieties abandoned, dispossessed of any remaining shyness, I gave of myself and took what I wanted in return. I felt both enslaved and emancipated, servant and master of the double-backed beast I'd created with this quiet, sensitive man. The pace and depth of his thrusts increased and I responded by wrapping my legs around him, pressing him into me, deeper and deeper. After changing position – first with me on top, cowgirl-style, then on all fours like a bitch in season – I lay on my back once again with Pierre between my thighs. His breathing quickened, each shallow breath snatched through gritted teeth; was he approaching his journey's end? No, not yet, I said to myself, wait for me, please! As if by some weird telepathy, it appeared that my thoughts had been received; Pierre's thrusting relented and the allegro pace relaxed into an easy adagio. This new movement, slower and less penetrating, only intensified the sensations in my groin. I delved into the space between us to stroke and gently rub the place where our bodies joined. I closed my eyes, carried on a cresting chemical wave of endorphins to the point of no return. We arrived at our orgasmic destination together, gasping for breath in the now stifling air, gazing at each other wide-eyed, intoxicated, sated and fulfilled. Pierre rolled over on his back and we lay together, side-by-side, fingers interlinked, staring up at the oak ceiling above us, listening to the chatter of the finches in the wisteria beyond the window.

Only then did we speak, and I realised that this day marked the conclusion of a long, long courtship. My feelings for Pierre predated the attack in the vineyard, the night at the opera, even the time I was shot in the neck the year before last. I'd been fond of him for longer than that, perhaps ever since our meeting at Fontloube on another September day three years ago. Today's romantic events were an affirmation of our love, an unspoken pledge, a contract signed beneath a weeping willow, sealed with a mutual climax and delivered with three little words.

'I love you.'

'*Je t'aime.*'

I've always envied male body confidence – the way a man can lose all physical inhibitions once the bumps and blemishes have been revealed. For men – in my limited experience – to bare all is to pardon all, and Pierre was no exception. While dressing, he strutted naked round the bedroom like a farmyard cockerel. I, on the other hand, grabbed my clothes and escaped to the privacy of the bathroom to shower and change.

When I re-emerged he was sitting on the bed pretending to read a copy of *Wuthering Heights*. I slipped on a pair of comfortable flat-heeled ballerina shoes and gave myself the once-over in the full-length mirror. Not bad, I thought, but not great either.

'Pierre?'

'Mmm?'

'How do I look in these shoes?'

'Lovely.'

185

'Not a bit . . . overweight?'

He seemed shocked at the suggestion. 'Not at all! You have a great figure, Jeanne. I used to think you were ten years younger than me, you know? I think those vines must keep you fit.'

'Well, I'm sure I could lose a kilo or two.'

He put the book down on the bedside table. 'Jeanne,' he said. 'You have a wonderful body. Curvaceous and feminine. Do you want to look like a supermodel? Believe me, most men – myself included – do not find skinny women attractive, whatever you read in all those fashion magazines.'

Unconvinced, I glanced over my shoulder at my bottom and legs, then peered at my face in the glass. 'Well, these lines on my face certainly give away my age – vineyard work is terrible for the complexion.'

'What? Those little goose's feet? Don't be ridiculous – they are the little imperfections that make you beautiful. It's like Loubna says: God's perfection is revealed through Man's imperfections . . . or something like that.'

I felt a needle-prick of jealousy and responded reflexively. 'When have you been talking to Loubna?'

His eyes did not leave mine. 'Well, on Thursday night, of course,' he said, smiling.

'Well,' I said, making light of my near-accusation, 'I'll have to watch her from now on!'

Pierre continued to smile. 'Come here, Jeanne. I want to tell you something.'

I approached the bed and sat down next to him.

'I don't go for skinny women. I don't go for beauty queens. And I don't go for girls half my age.'

'No surprise you ended up with me then!' I said, poking him in the ribs.

He grabbed me round the waist, pulled me to him and kissed me on the mouth.

'*Jeanne*,' he said, doing a decent impression of Wendy, '*you are a gorgeous girl!* Now, get a move on – we need to be at the Tour du Roi in twenty minutes.'

'Okay,' I said. 'By the way, it's crow's feet, not goose's.'

'So,' I said, buckling up in the front seat of the 308, 'now you can tell me what Lemaitre and Foliot said.

He slipped the clutch and pulled out into the lane. 'Confidentially?'

'Of course.'

'Well, Lemaitre has admitted telling Grouazel to put pressure on Rougeard, but he denies any involvement in the murder, or your attack.'

'Do you believe him?'

'His story is credible.'

'Which is?'

We waited at the junction of the D670, the right indicator clicking. When the traffic cleared, Pierre pulled out and put his foot down.

'It goes like this: Lemaitre hired Grouazel three years ago to work at the casino – caretaker, bodyguard, bouncer. After 2008 the car franchise and the wine company were both struggling and his lines of credit were running out. He began using Grouazel to call in a few debts, you know: gorilla-in-a-suit-type duties. At about the same time La Girondine won a contract to supply the American company, and Lemaitre thought his credit problems were over. The Americans couldn't get enough of his Saint-Emilion wine. But there was a problem.'

'Let me guess: supply couldn't keep up with demand?'

'*Exact*. When the Yanks ordered ten million bottles, he was faced with a dilemma. Either refuse the order and go bankrupt, or find a suitable replacement. He chose the latter, but didn't tell MidWest what was in the shipment. They were sold a *chat en poche* – how do you say "a cat in the pocket"?'

'A pig in a poke,' I said.

He looked at me dubiously. 'Okay, a pig in a poke. So, in 2009 he got his *négotiant*, François Deguelle, to buy up all the best ordinary Bordeaux wine this side of the Dordogne. You know the rest.'

'But how did Rougeard get involved?'

Pierre chuckled. 'Oh, you will love this. Rougeard had been supplying La Girondine for many years, and Franky Deguelle was a regular visitor at Château Lacasse. One day in spring, probably after a good lunch, he went to see Rougeard to confirm the year's order. It seems he left his laptop on Rougeard's desk. By the time he'd turned round to come back for it, René Rougeard had read the infamous email and forwarded a copy to himself.'

'Gosh,' I said. 'He wasn't stupid then?'

'Apparently he was an odious man, but not stupid, no. After that he began blackmailing Lemaitre – demanding higher prices for his wine, a new car, perks at the casino. When, finally, his demands were too much for Lemaitre to swallow, Grouazel was called in to retrieve the email evidence and threaten Rougeard.'

'Threaten?'

Pierre shrugged. 'I buy it,' he said. 'I think that circumstances changed everything. Rougeard refused to give Grouazel the computer and a fight broke out. Rougeard did not stand a chance, and you know well what happened to him. After witnessing the fight in the bar, Grouzel thought he could frame Hakim Watter. According to Lemaitre, he and Grouazel parted company the night we went to visit the casino; the assassin became the blackmailer.'

'God, I knew it was him. I saw him on the way back to the car park, and again on Thursday night after the *méchoui.*'

'It's possible. Before Friday he was lying low in his white van, until he bumped into you at the docks, of course. After that he went to see Lemaitre again.'

'Oh, my, God – he gave Grouazel my address!'

'Grouazel had already been tipped-off about the lady in the 2CV by Le Blaireau. When he saw you at the docks you went straight to the top of his hit-list. Lemaitre, blackmailed and threatened at knifepoint, was forced to disclose your address.'

I knew what that was like. 'I guess we'll never know if he's lying?'

'No, but Foliot knew what was going on when he disappeared to Nice.'

I felt queezy.

'What exactly was his involvement?'

'The killer forced him to plant the evidence, you know, the white overalls, and he'd given him an ultimatum too: charge Hakim Wattar or face scandal, dismissal and prison when the documents he was keeping were revealed. When Grouazel went after you, Foliot wanted to put as much distance as possible between himself and the case.'

'But what about the fraud – they are being investigated, right?'

'Commissaire Lamarque threatened them both with charges of culpable homicide and conspiracy. So, Lemaitre agreed to cooperate in the fraud investigation and attest to Foliot's involvement – if all allegations relating to the murder were dropped.'

'Wow. And they will be prosecuted? I mean, for the fraud.'

'If what we suspect is true, they will both go to prison, yes. By the way, it's only a matter of time before your involvement in this becomes known to the press.'

'I know. Lamarque told me quite sternly not to talk to anyone.'

'Yes, he's like that.'

We arrived in Saint-Emilion with only minutes to spare and parked as near to the King's Tower as Pierre could get us in the marked police car. I saw a line of red-robed members filing into the building. Those at the head of the procession had already arrived at the summit and were waving their red hats at the crowd gathered below. I jogged over to the building and joined the queue behind the American actor. At the door he stepped to the side to allow me to go before him.

'No, after you, please,' I said.

His movie-star face brightened. 'You're British!' he said.

''Fraid so.'

'Cool!' he said, preceding me into the echoey, cool interior of the tower. 'You know, it's good to talk English with someone – I've been struggling with my terrible French all day long.'

'I heard you earlier. You speak pretty good French.'

'Jeez, I wish you were right. I don't get all that masculine feminine stuff. And those verb endings!'

'It gets easier, but it takes time. My first vintage was '87 and I still get confused with the subjunctive.'

'Wow, you must be the English winemaker I've heard all about. I believe you're quite a personality! I'm David, by the way.'

'Jeanne,' I said, shaking hands, 'Jeanne Valeix. But I thought you were—?'

'Oh, that's just my stage name,' he said, a little out of breath now. 'Jeez these steps! You can call me David.'

'Okay, David,' I said, trying to suppress a grin.

'What is it?' he said, also smiling.

'Well,' I said, 'you're the personality. I'm just an ordinary *vigneronne*.'

'Uh-huh? I heard you and one of your team took down a wanted murderer. You're a goddamn hero!'

We came out into the soft evening light and took our appointed positions on the parapet. The ceremony began. David glanced at me. 'There's nothing ordinary about you, Jeanne, believe me.'

My cheeks turned as red as my silly hat and someone handed me what looked like an enormous bunch of grapes – a dozen-or-so black, helium-filled balloons tied together with string.

The words of the speech passed me by as I looked down at the crowd to see Wendy, Archie and Loubna, their faces tilted, eyes squinting into the light, waving and cheering. John Clare, Hakim Wattar and a pair of Doberman pinschers arrived and joined the group. I spotted Pierre and Lieutenant Dauzac to the side of the crowd, clapping and smiling. I gazed out over Saint-Emilion's pan-tiled roofs and tracked the flight of a pair of buzzards, circling on the thermals above a thousand hectares of vines.

David touched my arm. 'You can let go now,' he said.

I unclenched my fist and watched the giant grapes sail up and away into the sky.

Janvier 2012

So, that was it. That was how we solved René Rougeard's murder, how we uncovered the shameful wine scam, and how I eventually found happiness. The lonely Widow Valeix of Château Fontloube now has a partner (of sorts) as well as her faithful Jack Russell terrier, a couple of dependent twenty-somethings and an elderly surrogate mother. It's a far from conventional family, but I'm a far from conventional girl. And not a girl anymore – I'll be forty-seven this year. Perhaps it's time to start taking it easy, doing a bit less of the physical side of winemaking. Certainly, with the court case beginning in February I shan't be able to do much of the pruning and trellising this year; there'll be more work than usual for Archie and Loubna to do. Maybe my calloused hands will soften during the hours I'll be spending in the witness box. In fact, there are two judicial proceedings for me to attend: the prosecutions of Victor Lemaitre, Xavier Foliot and François Deguelle for the Thomas Jefferson's Cellar wine fraud, and Le Baireau's trial at the *tribunal d'instance* later this month for benefit fraud and receiving stolen goods. I have no sympathy for any of them, but the Badger's conviction will give me less satisfaction than the others – at the very least our encounter in the bar PMU has given me an amusing dinner-party anecdote.

And what of Captain – now *Commandant* – Lefèvre? Well, he and I have a mutually satisfactory arrangement. We can't live together, but neither do we want to stop seeing each other. He has his life; I have mine. And the times we spend in each other's company are all the more enjoyable for it. Wendy calls him my boyfriend, and I like that. She's teaching Hakim to speak English, and they've both vowed to stay off the booze for the whole of January. Sometimes miracles happen, don't they? After John Clare's harvest I introduced him to Lieutenant Dauzac, and the two of them seem to have hit it off. Loubna and Archie are still as inseparable from each other as they are from their gangster movie DVDs. And as for my movie star acquaintance, David, he sent us all signed photographs and vowed to visit Fontloube one day. I wonder if he'll keep his word.

End.

The Grape's Joy

by Patrick Hilyer

"a real page turner of a story full of teasing clues and cliff-hanging suspense...a triumph of a little book, immensely readable and with the added interest of its back-story for the wine buff. Highly recommended."
Tom Cannavan, wine journalist

"This is a book I wanted to finish and yet was enjoying the journey so much that I forced myself to ration the chapters to make it last longer. I just hope this is the first of many such books from this very talented writer with a mastery of bitter-sweet tales."
Peter F May, Wine Editor, BellaOnline

"...full-bodied, spicy with fascinating and fruity overtones."
John Walker, Author of The Jagermeister's Apprentice

French Vineyards

by Patrick Hilyer

"a wonderful book, full of information and enchantment"
Heimburger's European Traveller

"great places to stay on French wine-producing estates,
from châteaux to B&Bs"
The Guardian

"a vicarious travel adventure"
Jancis Robinson OBE, Master of Wine

"enticing and indispensable"
Jonathan Ray, wines editor, Daily Telegraph

"recommendations from all the French wine regions" Jim
Budd, independent wine journalist and chairman of
The Circle of Wine Writers

Printed in Poland
by Amazon Fulfillment
Poland Sp. z o.o., Wrocław

57546646R00114